STRANDED

STRANDED

V. L. McDermid

Foreword by Ian Rankin

First published in Great Britain in 2005 by Flambard Press
Stable Cottage, East Fourstones, Hexham NE47 5DX
Reprinted in 2005

Typeset by BookType
Cover design by Gainford Design Associates
Front-cover photograph by the author
Author photograph by Mimsy Moller
Printed in England by Cromwell Press, Trowbridge, Wiltshire

A CIP catalogue record for this book is available from the British Library

ISBN 1 873226 74 8 (paperback)
ISBN 1873226 76 4 (hardback)

Flambard Press wishes to thank Arts Council England for its financial support.

website: www.flambardpress.co.uk

Flambard Press is a member of Inpress and Independent Northern Publishers.

Acknowledgements

The stories in this collection were first published as follows:

'Mittel' in *Europride Anthology* (Comma Press, 2003)

'The Wagon Mound' in *Good Housekeeping* (2002)

'Driving a Hard Bargain' in *The Mail on Sunday* (1996)

'Breathtaking Ignorance' in *The Crazy Jig* (Polygon, 1996)

'White Nights, Black Magic' in *Crime in the City* (Do-Not Press, 2002)

'The Writing on the Wall' in *3rd Culprit* (Chatto & Windus, 1994)

'Keeping on the Right Side of the Law' in *The City Life Book of Manchester Stories* (Penguin, 1999)

'A Wife in a Million' in *Reader, I Murdered Him* (The Women's Press, 1989)

'A Traditional Christmas' in *Reader, I Murdered Him Too* (The Women's Press, 1994)

'The Girl Who Killed Santa Claus' in the *News of the World* magazine (2000)

'Sneeze for Danger', commissioned and broadcast by BBC Radio 4 (2004)

'Guilt Trip' in *No Alibi* (Ringpull Press, 1995)

'Homecoming' in *Endangered Species* (Arts Council online anthology, 2004)

'Heartburn' in *Northern Blood 2* (Flambard Press, 1995)

'Four Calling Birds' in *12 Days* (Virago, 2004)

'The Consolation Blonde' in *Mysterious Pleasures* (Little, Brown, 2003)

'Metamorphosis' in *Tart Noir* (Picador, 2002)

'When Larry Met Allie' in *The New English Library Book of Internet Stories* (New English Library, 2000)

'The Road and the Miles to Dundee', commissioned by New Writing North in 2004 and previously unpublished

Contents

Foreword

Passion. Obsession. Revenge.

These three words would make a great tag-line on a movie poster, and they are subjects Val McDermid tackles in her short stories. The mark of great short-story writers, however, is that they not only unsettle their readers, shaking us out of complacency, but that they explore the psychology of human interaction. In his book of modern aphorisms, *The Book of Shadows*, the poet Don Paterson includes the following: 'A mercy, I suppose, that it ended. Any deeper intimacy with each other's anatomy would have involved a murder.'

Val McDermid could almost have written those words, including that wry and tangy 'I suppose'. Of course, in Val's world things often go far beyond Don Paterson's imaginings, because the crime-writer recognises that love is the most destructive of emotions. It turns worlds upside down and people inside out. It can so easily turn to lust, or envy, or loathing. It can, and often does, lead to violence, both emotional and physical.

Val has always been a restless writer – the journey through her fictional universe could never have been made by a single, consistent hero or heroine – and the short-story form suits her, allowing her to pick apart relationships with a furious skill, highlighting flaws and jealousies. The readers can see tragedy and horror emerging while the participants cannot. And always there are those twists awaiting us, just when we think we've seen it all. But Val is no fatalist: a dark humour infuses many of the stories here, and one story – 'The Road and the Miles to Dundee' – is very different to the others, allowing the author to explore her roots and the strong pull of family and background. It's a hugely moving tale and one which shows her extraordinary range.

Those who have read her novel *Killing the Shadows* will be unsurprised that Val has a dark view of the writer's life, exhibited here in no fewer than four stories. Her writers harbour dark secrets or painful memories, or are driven to act out revenge tragedies not dissimilar to the ones they write about. I only hope I never get on her wrong side . . .

I should, right at the start, have laid my cards on the table. I've known Val for years. But before I knew her, I knew her books. I was intrigued by the author biography on her early jackets. It seemed to me we must have grown up near one another. And so we did: five miles apart, yet we first met in Seattle, where we were both attending a crime-fiction convention. We went out drinking and talking and – eventually – singing. Since then, we've shared experiences which would make decent short stories in themselves . . . except that few people would believe them. The short story, after all, unlike real life, has to convince us that it could have happened, or might be happening right now. And this is the real trick of a good short story: it has to pull us into its world straight away, convincing us with immediately recognisable characters. Once snared, we can begin our descent into the dark confines of the plot.

There are stories here which will make you shudder, and which will linger long in the mind. Tiny worlds of hurt and healing: the hurt we do to each other; the healing that comes with recognition. The recognition that we have these potentials within us. It's up to us to choose between good and evil, love and destruction.

Ian Rankin

Mittel

Picture a city, its architecture a mix of Austro-Hungarian empire and former Eastern bloc. A mix that should sit uneasily together but instead fits comfortably from long familiarity. Picture this city, its long strings of trams dominating wide streets that feel dusty but which are in fact surprisingly clean. Picture this city, its inhabitants going about their imaginable business, their pace brisker than by the Mediterranean but more sultry than in its colder northern sisters. Picture this city. Call it Mittel.

And in this city, a street. And in this street, a café. And in this café, a table. And at this table, a woman. And in her hand, a pen.

What she is writing is not important. It is not part of the lesson she has to teach you. The fact that she is writing at a table, alone, however, is part of that lesson.

You have spent years living with a different woman, one who never understood that when you were irritable or impatient it was seldom with her. It was simply your way of externalising other stresses, other frustrations. And it made you crazy, her inability not to take this personally.

And now the wheel has turned and you are in love with a woman who is sometimes distant and shrouded. And you are slowly grasping the fact that this is seldom anything to do with you. It is simply her way of externalising other stresses, other frustrations. And you are having to learn not to take

13

this personally.

You walk up to the table in the café in the street in the city of Mittel after the agreed length of time has passed. And now the sun is out. Her smile dazzles you with its warmth. And suddenly the tumblers click, the juggler hangs seven balls in the air and you know you've done the right thing. 'Perfect timing,' she says.

Yes, you think. But it doesn't last. Every time you take a run at it, your feet stumble on unexpected cobbles. And there's always a good reason for it, a reason that makes perfect sense to both of you, but a reason that still leaves you feeling bleached and split like driftwood on the shores of love.

At last, you call her on it. 'Is everything all right between us?'

Apparently surprised, she says, 'Of course it is.'

'Only, you haven't touched me since we got here. I'm not talking about sex, I'm talking about just touching me, kissing me, holding me.'

'You know I'm not comfortable with public displays of affection.'

'I know that. But I'm talking about when we're here together, in bed, in our room, in the hotel. By ourselves.'

'I'm nervous about my presentation today,' she says. 'And I'm tired. And this bed's uncomfortable. And it's hot. And I'm premenstrual. And I find it hard to combine work and pleasure. And it's not fair, I'm not even awake.' And she turns away because she doesn't want to feel your eyes on her.

You tell her you love her. She grunts, 'Love you too.'

So you keep your distance all day. You leave her to talk to everybody else, to dazzle them with her discourse, which she does supremely well. You notice this, in spite of your efforts not to let her feel you're scrutinising her. You stay back, out of her face, give her space. And at last, at the end of the afternoon, you're back at the hotel, there's the prospect of a couple of hours together before the evening marathon of more presentations in languages neither of you speak.

Listen to this. A city where the low boom of church bells calling the hours is lost in the rattle of rain on café awnings. Breathe this. A city whose market square is heavy with the perfume of strawberries and lavender. Imagine this. A city where wars have left recent scars and where history is alive and kicking, where conversations turn to conflicts on the turn of a nuance. And in this city, a hotel. And in this hotel, a room. And in this room, a woman. She's standing behind you, fingers tentative on your shoulder blades. You wish to fuck she'd stop it. You told her right at the start that you don't do reassurance. Your self-sufficiency makes you impatient of neediness. And today, with an unnamed anxiety gnawing at you, making her feel better isn't something you're capable of.

You love this woman. You've opened yourself up to possibilities with her. You don't do commitment, but you've committed to her by the simple – but for you, infinitely complicated – act of telling the people you care about that you're with her and you're happy. But sometimes you wish she was a million miles away. She's easier to love at a distance when her need surfaces and makes demands on you that you don't want to meet. Sure, you are touched by her pain. And there are times when you are proud to be the one that this strong woman is willing to be vulnerable with. But sometimes it's just too damn hard.

You know you're not always fair to her. She'd pay whatever it took to love you, and all you're required to do is to make a space in your life big enough for part-time love. But she's not a small, insignificant person. She's big in every way and she's already carved a niche in your world. Her name follows you round at work and at play. Her face insinuates itself at unlikely and unpredictable points in your daily existence. You turn on the radio and her voice fills the room. And sometimes her ubiquity even in her absence feels like suffocation, her very generosity a trap.

You want this to work, more than you've wanted anything for a long time. You want what she brings in her gift – reliability, intelligence, good humour and a sense of a future that contains what you both want. And you do want so many of the same things; truly, you do. You know because you've both spent a long time working them out before either of you even knew that you would end up letting this love breathe.

But still you shrug away from the stroke of her fingers. Just a tiny movement, almost imperceptible but enough for her to get the message. From the corner of your peripheral vision, you see her hand jerk back.

'What do you want to do?' you say. 'It's probably too late in the day for a museum or a gallery. We could go back up to the old town. Or look at shoe shops.' This last with a grin. You know her weakness for footwear.

'I don't care,' she says. 'This is the last time we'll have alone together for ages. I don't mind what we do. I'd be happy to stand on a street corner in the rain as long as I'm with you.'

You know she means it. You picture the two of you locked

in an embrace on the busy corner of the street, oblivious to the trams clattering past, the traffic cop dressed in white directing the cars and buses, the umbrellas parting around you as the rain pours down, plastering your hair to your head, running in rivulets down the inside of the collar of your leather jacket. You imagine the tender warmth of her lips against yours, the feel of her body soft against the stiff leather, and you know you love her enough to do it too.

'OK,' you say. 'Let's go.'

And then she reaches for you, hands at your waist, eyes pleading. And it's gone, the dream of love in the rain on the street corner.

Your hands flutter up in a defensive gesture. 'I'm not . . . I can't . . . I'm not in the right place for this.'

You see the hurt she tries to hide and you hate the way she can make you feel bad for nothing more than being who you are.

Out in the street, the rain falls relentlessly. Two blocks from the hotel, she stops abruptly and says she doesn't want to walk. 'You go off and do your thing,' she says. 'I'll catch up with you at the presentation.'

You smile. It's a real smile and you see that register in her eyes. And suddenly, surprisingly, she's smiling too. And her smile is a mirror of yours in its genuineness.

And that's when you understand it might just be fine.

Picture a city. A city whose tacky souvenirs include a pair of wooden figures sheltering under an umbrella. A city where statues of heroes are turned to face the direction of the latest enemy. A city that tries not to wear its hurt on its sleeve. Picture this city. Call it Mittel.

Driving a Hard Bargain

I'd find it a lot easier to believe in therapists if they acknowledged the existence of the inner spiv as well as the inner child, parent, teacher and washing-machine mechanic. We've all got one, and no matter how hard we try to be stylish and sophisticated, our inner spiv will sabotage us every time. It's the driving force that dictates Prince Charles's cuff links and Hugh Grant's sexual hot button.

I share my weakness with Princess Diana. No, I'm not talking bleating, indiscreet me. I'm talking motors. But it's not the big Mercs and the turbocharged Bentleys that speak to the spiv in me. It's flashy cabriolets, sleek feline coupés that make teenage boys on street corners drool. Tragically, these days, like sex for men with XXXX-large beer guts, it's all in the mind. The one drawback to my chosen career as Kate Brannigan, private eye, is that when it comes to cruising the mean streets of Manchester, it's anonymity that cuts it, not flamboyance.

A girl can still dream, though. So when Gerry Banks told me he'd lost his BMW Z3 roadster, one of only half a dozen then in the country, an advance release that had cost him a small fortune to come by and which turned every head when he drove down the street, I understood why he spoke as if he was talking about the death of a particularly close and beloved family member. If I'd been lucky enough to own one of those little beauties, I'd have probably replaced the bedroom wall with an up-and-over door so I could sleep with it. And if some rat had kidnapped my baby and held it to ransom, I'd have hired every investigator in the kingdom if it meant bringing my darling home to me.

Banks had revealed his pain behind the closed door of his office, a functional box on the upper floor of the custom-built factory where his company made state-of-the-art electronic components. The sort of things that tell your tumble drier exactly when to scorch your favourite shirt. The best you could call the view of the nearby M62 would be 'uninspiring'. But if, like Gerry Banks, all you could see was a hole in the car park where a scarlet roadster ought to be, it must have been heartbreaking.

'I take it that's the scene of the crime,' I said, joining him by the window.

He pointed to the empty parking space nearest the door, the series of smooth curves that made up his pudgy features rearranging themselves into corrugated lines. 'Bastard,' was all he said.

I waited for a couple of minutes, the way you do when someone's paying their respects to the dead. When I spoke, my voice was gentle. 'I'm going to need full details.'

'Fine,' he sighed, turning away and throwing himself miserably into his black leather executive chair. I was left with the bog-standard visitor's number in charcoal tweed and tubular metal. Just in case I didn't know who was the boss here.

'Take me through it from the beginning,' I urged when he showed no signs of communicating further.

'He turned up on Tuesday morning at nine. He said his name was John Wilkins and he ran an executive valet service for cars. He gave me a business card and a glossy brochure. It quotes half a dozen top Manchester businessmen saying what a great job this Valet-While-U-Work does.' His voice was the self-justifying whine of a man desperate not to be seen as the five-star prat he'd been. He pushed a folded A4 sheet towards me, a business card lying on top of it. I gave them the brief glance that was all they deserved. Nothing that couldn't come out of any neighbourhood print shop.

'So you agreed to let him valet your car?'

He nodded. 'I gave him the keys and he promised to have it back by close of business. But he didn't.' He clenched his jaw, bunching the muscles under his ear.

'And that's when you got the fax?'

He looked away, ostensibly searching for the piece of paper I knew was right under his hand. 'Here,' he said.

'We've got your car. By this time Friday, you'll have ten thousand pounds. Fair exchange is no robbery. No cops or the car gets it just badly enough not to be a write-off. Yours faithfully, Rob-It-While-U-Work,' I read. A villain with a sense of humour. 'The price seems a bit steep,' I said. 'I thought the Z3 only cost about twenty grand new.'

'If you can get one. They're not officially released till next January and there's already a two-year waiting list. Money can't buy a replacement. I'm not interested in common rubbish. You know where I live? Not in some poxy executive development. I live in a converted sixteenth-century chapel. There's not another one like it in the world. Anywhere. I want my car back, you understand? Without a scratch on it,' Banks said, the ghost of his management skills starting to emerge from the shadows of his grief. 'I'll have the money here tomorrow afternoon, and I want you to take care of the exchange. Can you handle that?'

I'm so used to middle-aged businessmen taking one look at my twenty-nine-year-old five feet and three inches and treating me like the tea girl that it barely registers on the Brannigan scale of indignation any more. 'I can handle it,' I said mildly. 'But wouldn't you rather get the car back and hang on to the cash?'

'You think you could do that? Without putting the car at risk?'

I gave him the stare I'd copied from Al Pacino. 'I can try.'

Like journalists, private eyes are only as good as their sources. Unfortunately, our best ones tend to be people your mother would bar from the doorstep, never mind the house. Like my mechanic, Handbrake. He's no ordinary grease monkey. He learned his trade tuning up the wheels for a series of perfect getaways after his mates had relieved some financial institution of a wad they hadn't previously realized was surplus to requirements. He only got caught the once. That had been enough.

When he got out, he'd set himself up in a backstreet garage and gone straight. Ish. But he still knew who was who among the players on the wrong side of the fence. And as well as keeping my car nondescript on the outside and faster than a speeding bullet on the inside, he tipped me the odd wink on items he thought I might be interested in. It sat easier with his conscience than talking to Officer Dibble. He answered the phone just as I was about to give up. 'Yeah?' Time is money; chat is inessential.

'Handbrake, Brannigan.' The conversational style was

catching. 'I'm working for a punter who's had his BMW Z3 ripped for a ransom. The guy called himself John Wilkins. Valet-While-U-Work. Any ideas?'

'Dunno the name but there's a couple of teams have tried it on,' he told me. 'A Z3, you say? I didn't think there were any over here yet.'

'There's only a handful, according to the punter.'

'Right. Rarity value, that's what makes it worth ransoming. Anything else, forget it – cheaper to let the car walk, cop for the insurance. I'll ask around, talk to the usual suspects, see what the word is.'

I started the engine and slipped the car into gear at about the same time my brain did the same thing. A couple of minutes later, I was grinning at Gerry Banks's receptionist for the second time that morning. 'Me again,' I chirped. Nothing like stating the obvious to make the victim of your interrogation feel superior.

'Mr Banks has gone into a meeting with a client,' she said in the bored singsong you need to master before they let you qualify as a receptionist.

'Actually, it was you I wanted a word with.' Ingratiating smile.

She looked startled. I'd obviously gone for a concept she was unfamiliar with.

'Why?'

'Mr Banks has hired me to try to get his car back,' I said. 'A couple of questions?'

She shrugged.

'When the car valet bloke arrived, did he ask who the Z3 belonged to?'

She shook her head. 'He said, could he have five minutes

with Mr Banks concerning the ongoing maintenance of his roadster. I buzzed Mr Banks, then sent him in.'

'Those were his actual words? He said roadster?'

'That's right. Like Mr Banks always calls it.'

I'd been afraid that's what she would say.

I was being ushered into the presence of my financial advisor when Handbrake rang me back. Josh waved me to one of his comfortable leather armchairs while I wrestled the phone out of my bag and to my ear. 'You got a problem I can't solve,' Handbrake said. 'Whoever's got your punter's motor, either they're not from around here or they're new talent. So new nobody knows who they are.'

'I had a funny feeling you were going to tell me that,' I said. 'I owe you one.'

'I'll add it to your next service.'

I hung up. This was beginning to look more and more like something very personal. 'Drink?' Josh asked sympathetically.

'I'm not stopping. This is just a quick smash-and-grab raid. Gerry Banks, Compuponents. Who's got it in for him?'

The only thing in common between Gerry Banks's home and the flat whose bell I was leaning on was that they'd both been converted. Somehow, I couldn't see my client in this scruffy Edwardian rat-trap in the hinterland between the curry restaurants of Rusholme and the street hookers of Whalley Range.

Eventually the door opened on a woman in jeans faded to the colour of her eyes, a baggy chenille jumper and her early thirties. Dark blonde hair was loosely pulled back in a pony-tail. She had the kind of face that makes men pause with their pints halfway to their lips. 'Yeah?' she asked.

'Tania Banks?'

Her head tilted to one side and two little lines appeared between her perfectly groomed eyebrows. 'Who wants to know?'

I held a business card at eye level. 'I've come about the car.'

The animation leaked out of her face like the air from a punctured tyre. 'I haven't got a car,' she said, her voice grating and cold.

'Neither has your husband.'

A muscle at the corner of her mouth twitched. 'I've got nothing to say.'

I shrugged. 'Please yourself. I thought we could leave the police out of it, but if you want to play it the other way . . .'

'You don't frighten me,' she lied.

'Maybe not, but I'm sure your husband knows people who would.'

Her shoulders sagged, her mouth slackened in defeat. 'You'd better come in.'

The bedsit was colder and damper than the street outside, in spite of the gas fire hissing at full blast. She perched on the bed, leaving the chair to me. 'You left him three months ago,' I said.

'I got tired of everybody feeling sorry for me. I got tired of him only ever coming home when the latest mistress was out of town on a modelling assignment,' she sighed, lighting a cheap cigarette.

'And you wanted a life. That's why you've been doing the

part-time law degree,' I said.

Her eyebrows flickered. 'I finished the degree. I've just started the one-year course you need to be a solicitor.'

'You don't get a grant.' Some of my best friends are lawyers; I know about these things. 'The fees are somewhere around four and a half grand. Plus you've got to have something to live on. Which you expected to get from the divorce settlement. Only, there's a problem, isn't there?'

'You're well informed,' she said.

'It's my job. He's clever with money, your husband. On paper, he's spotless. It's the offshore holding company that owns the car, the house, everything. He takes a salary of a few hundred a month. And the company pays for everything else. And it's all perfectly legal. On paper, he can't afford to pay you a shilling. So you decided to extract your divorce settlement by a slightly unorthodox route.'

She looked away, studying the hand that held the cigarette. 'Ten grand's a fraction of what I'm entitled to,' she said softly. Her admission of guilt didn't give me the usual adrenalin rush. She sighed again. 'You have no idea what I've had to put up with over the years.'

I submitted my account to Gerry Banks without a qualm. I'd done the job he asked me to do, and as far as I was concerned, he should be grateful. He'd asked me to handle the exchange, to make sure his car came back to him in one piece. It had been me who'd made the foolish offer to get the Z3 back without handing over the cash. And everybody knows that we women aren't up to the demanding job of being private eyes, don't they? Hardly surprising I wasn't able to live up to my promises.

Besides, we'll have forgotten each other inside six months. But I'll never forget the wind in my hair the night Tania Banks and my inner spiv cruised the M6 till dawn with the top down.

The *Wagon Mound*

Nothing destroys the quality of life so much as insomnia. Ask any parent of a new baby. It only takes a few broken nights to reduce the most calm and competent person to a twitching shadow of their normal proficiency. My wakefulness started when the nightmares began. When I did manage to drop off, the visions my subconscious mind conjured up were guaranteed to wake me, sweating and terrified, within a couple of hours of nodding off. It didn't take long before I began to fear sleep itself, dreading the demons that ripped through the fabric of my previous ease. I tried sleeping pills, I tried alcohol. But nothing worked.

I never dreamed that I'd rediscover the art of sleeping through the night thanks to a legal precedent. In 1961, the Privy Council heard a case concerning a negligent oil spillage from a ship called the *Wagon Mound* in Sydney Harbour. The oil fouled a nearby wharf, and in spite of expert advice that it wouldn't catch fire, when the wharf's owners began welding work, the oil did exactly what it wasn't supposed to do. The fire that followed caused enough damage for it to be worth taking to court, where the Privy Council finally decreed that the ship's owners weren't liable because the *type* of harm sustained by the plaintiff must itself be reasonably foreseeable. When Roger, the terminally boring commercial attaché at the Moscow Embassy, launched into the tale the other night in the bar at Proyekt OGI, he could never have imagined that it would change my life so dramatically. But then, lawyers have never been noted for their imagination.

Proximity. That's another legal principle that came up during Roger's lecture. How many intervening stages lie between cause and effect. I think by then I was the only one listening, because his disquisition had made me think back to the starting point of my sleepless nights.

Although the seeds were sown when my boss in London decided to invite the bestselling biographer Sam Uttley on a British Council tour of Russia, I can't be held accountable for that. The first point where I calculate I have to accept responsibility was on the night train from Moscow to St Petersburg.

I'd been looking after Sam ever since he'd landed at Sheremetyevo airport two days before. I hadn't seen him smile in all that time. He'd lectured lugubriously at the university, glumly addressed a gathering at the British Council library, done depressing signings at two bookshops and sulked his way round a reception at the Irish embassy. Even the weather seemed to reflect his mood, grey clouds lowering over Moscow and turning April into autumn. Minding visiting authors is normally the part of my job I like best, but spending time with Sam was about as much fun as having a hole in your shoe in a Russian winter. We'd all been hoping for some glamour from Sam's visit; his Channel Four series on the roots of biography had led us to expect a glowing Adonis with twinkling eyes and a gleaming grin. Instead, we got a glowering black dog.

Over dinner on the first evening, he'd downed his vodka like a seasoned Russian hand, and gloomed like the most depressive Slav in the Caucasus. On the short walk back to his hotel, I asked him if everything was all right. 'No,' he said shortly. 'My wife's just left me.'

Right, I thought. Don't go there, Sarah. 'Oh,' I think I said.

The final event of his Moscow visit was a book signing, and afterwards I took him to dinner to pass the time till midnight, when the train would leave for St Pete's. That was when the floodgates opened. He was miserable, he admitted. He was terrible company. But Rachel had walked out on him after eight years of marriage. There wasn't anyone else, she'd said. It was just that she was bored with him, tired of his celebrity, fed up of feeling inferior intellectually. I pointed out that these reasons seemed somewhat contradictory.

He brightened up at that. And suddenly the sun came out. He acted as if I'd somehow put my finger on something that should make him feel better about the whole thing. He radiated light, and I basked in the warmth of his smile. Before long, we were laughing together, telling our life stories, swapping intimacies. Flirting, I suppose.

We boarded the train a little before midnight, each dumping our bags in our separate first-class compartments. Then Sam produced a bottle of Georgian champagne from his holdall. 'A nightcap?' he suggested.

'Why not?' I was in the mood, cheered beyond reason by the delights of his company. He sat down on the sleeping berth beside me, and it seemed only natural when his arm draped across my shoulders. I remember the smell of him; a dark, masculine smell with an overlay of some spicy cologne with an edge of cinnamon. If I'm honest, I was willing him to kiss me before he actually did. I was entirely disarmed by his charm. But I also felt sorry for the pain that had been so obvious over the previous two days. And maybe, just maybe, the inherent *Doctor Zhivago* romance of the night train tipped the balance.

I don't usually do this kind of thing. What am I saying? I *never* do this kind of thing. In four years of chasing around after authors, or having them chase after me, I'd not given into temptation once. But Sam penetrated all of my professional defences, and I moaned under his hands from Moscow to St Petersburg. By morning, he swore I'd healed his heart. By the time he left St Pete's three days later, we'd arranged to meet in London, where I was due to attend a meeting in ten days' time. I'd been out of love for a long time; it wasn't hard to fall for a man who was handsome, clever and amusing, and who seemed to find me irresistible.

Two days' later, I got his first e-mail. I'd been checking every waking hour on the hour, wondering and edgy. It turned out I had good reason to be anxious. The e-mail was short and sour.

> Dear Sarah, Rachel and I have decided we want to try to resolve our difficulties. It'll come as no surprise to you that my marriage is my number one priority. So I think it best if we don't communicate further. Sorry if this seems cold, but there's no other way to say it. Sam.

I was stunned. This wasn't cold, it was brutal. A hard jab below the ribs, designed to take my breath away and deflect any possible comeback. I felt the physical shock in the pit of my stomach.

Of course, I blamed myself for my stupidity, my eagerness to believe that a man as charismatic as Sam could fall for me.

Good old reliable Sarah, the safe pair of hands who second-guessed authors' needs before they could even voice them. I felt such a fool. A bruised, exploited fool.

Time passed, but there was still a raw place deep inside me. Sam Uttley had taken more from me than a few nights of sexual pleasure; he'd taken away my trust in my judgement. I told nobody about my humiliation. It would have been one pain too many.

Then Lindsay McConnell arrived. An award-winning dramatist, she'd come to give a series of workshops on radio adaptation. She was impeccably professional, no trouble to take care of. And we hit it off straightaway. On her last night, I took her to my favourite Moscow eating place, a traditional Georgian restaurant tucked away in a courtyard in the Armenian quarter. As the wine slipped down, we gossiped and giggled. Then, in the course of some anecdote, she mentioned Sam Uttley. Just hearing his name made my guts clench. 'You know Sam?' I asked, struggling not to sound too interested.

'Oh God, yes. I was at university with Rachel, his wife. Of course, you had Sam out here last year, didn't you? He said he'd had a really interesting time.'

I bet he did, I thought bitterly. 'How are they now? Sam and Rachel?' I asked with the true masochist's desire for the twist of the knife.

Lindsay looked puzzled. 'What do you mean, how are they now?'

'When Sam was here, Rachel had just left him.'

She frowned. 'Are you sure you're not confusing him with someone else? They're solid as a rock, Sam and Rachel. God knows, if he was mine I'd have murdered him years ago, but

Rachel thinks the sun shines out of his arse.'

It was my turn to frown. 'He told me she'd just walked out on him. He was really depressed about it.'

Lindsay shook her head. 'God, how very Sam. He hates touring, you know. He'll do anything to squeeze out a bit of sympathy, make sure he gets premier-league treatment. He just likes to have everyone running around after him, Sarah. I'm telling you, Rachel has never left him. Now I think about it, that week he was in Russia, I went round there for dinner. Me and Rachel and a couple of her colleagues. You know, from *Material Girl*. The magazine she works for. I think if they'd split up, she might have mentioned it, don't you?'

I hoped I wasn't looking as stunned as I felt. I'd never thought of myself as stupid, but that calculating bastard had spun me a line and reeled me in open-mouthed like the dumbest fish in the pond. But of course, because I'm a woman and that's how we're trained to think, I was still blaming myself more than him. I'd clearly been sending out the signals of needy gullibility and he'd just come up with the right line to exploit them.

A few weeks later, I was still smarting from what I saw as my self-inflicted wound at the Edinburgh Book Festival, where us British Council types gather like bees to pollen. But at least I'd finally have the chance to share my idiocy with Camilla, my opposite number in Jerusalem. We'd worked together years before in Paris, and we'd become bosom buddies. The only reason I hadn't told her about Sam previously was that every time I wrote it down in an e-mail, it just looked moronic. It needed a girls' night in with a couple of bottles of decent red wine before I could let this one spill out.

Late on the second night, after a particularly gruelling Amnesty International event, we sneaked back to the flat we were sharing with a couple of the boys from the Berlin office and started in on the confessional. My story crawled out of me, and I realised yet again how foolish I'd been from the horrified expression on Camilla's face. That and her appalled silence. 'I don't believe it,' she breathed.

'I know, I know,' I groaned. 'How could I have been so stupid?'

'No, no,' she said angrily. 'Not you, Sarah. Sam Uttley.'

'What?'

'That duplicitous bastard Uttley. He pulled exactly the same stunt on Georgie Bullen in Madrid. The identical line about his wife leaving him. She told me about it when I flew in for *Semana Negra* last month.'

'But I thought Georgie was living with someone?'

'She was,' Camilla said. 'Paco, the stage manager at the opera house. She'd taken Uttley down to Granada to do some lectures there, that's when it happened. Georgie saw the scumbag off on the plane and came straight home and told Paco it was over, she'd met someone else. She threw him out, then two days later she got the killer e-mail from Sam.'

We gazed at each other, mouths open. 'The bastard,' I said. For the first time, anger blotted out my self-pity and pain.

'Piece of shit,' Camilla agreed.

We spent the rest of the bottle and most of the second one thinking of ways to exact revenge on Sam Uttley, but we both knew that there was no way I was going back to Moscow to find a hit man to take him out. The trouble was, we couldn't think of anything that would show him up without making us look like silly credulous girls. Most blokes, no matter how much they might pretend otherwise, would reckon: good on him for working out such a foolproof scam to get his leg over. Most women would reckon we'd got what we deserved for being so naïve.

I was thirty thousand feet above Poland when the answer came to me. The woman in the seat next to me had been reading *Material Girl* and she offered it to me when she'd finished. I looked down the editorial list, curious to see exactly what Rachel Uttley did on the magazine. Her name was near the top of the credits. *Fiction editor, Rachel Uttley.* A quick look at the contents helped me deduce that, as well as the books page, Rachel was responsible for editing the three short stories. There, at the end of the third, was a sentence saying that submissions for publication should be sent to her.

I've always wanted to write. One of the reasons I took this job in the first place was to learn as much as I could from those who do it successfully. I've got half a novel on my hard disk, but I reckoned it was time to try a short story.

Two days later, I'd written it. The central character was a biographer who specialises in seducing professional colleagues on foreign trips with a tale about his wife having left him. Then he'd dump them as soon as he'd got home. When one of his victims realises what he's been up to, she exposes the serial adulterer by sending his wife, a magazine editor, a short story revealing his exploits. And the wife, recognising her errant husband from the pen portrait, finally does walk out on him.

Before I could have second thoughts, I printed it out and stuffed it in an envelope addressed to Rachel at *Material*

Girl. Then I sat back and waited.

For a couple of weeks, nothing happened.

Then, one Tuesday morning, I was sitting in the office browsing BBC online news. His name leapt out at me. 'Sam Uttley Dies in Burglary', read the headline in the latest-news section. I clicked on the <more> button.

> Bestselling biographer and TV presenter Sam Uttley was found dead this morning at his home in North London. It is believed he disturbed a burglar. He died from a single stab wound to the stomach. Police say there was evidence of a break-in at the rear of the house.
>
> Uttley was discovered by his wife, Rachel, a journalist. Police are calling for witnesses who may have seen one or two men fleeing the scene in the early hours of the morning.

I had to read the bare words three or four times before they sank in. Suddenly, his lies didn't matter any more. All I could think of was his eyes on mine, the flash of his easy smile, the touch of his hand. The sparkle of wit in his conversation. The life in him that had been snuffed out. The books he would never write.

Over a succession of numb days, I pursued the story via the internet. Bits and pieces emerged gradually. They'd had an attempted burglary a few months before. That night, Rachel had gone off to bed but Sam had stayed up late, working in his study. Sam, the police reckoned, had heard the sound of breaking glass and gone downstairs to investigate. The intruder had snatched up a knife from the kitchen worktop and plunged it into his stomach then fled. Sam had bled to death on the kitchen floor. It had taken him a while to die, they thought. And Rachel had come down for breakfast to find him stiff and cold. Poor bloody Rachel, I thought.

On the fifth day after the news broke, there was a large manila envelope among my post, franked with the *Material Girl* logo. My story had come winging its way back to me. Inside, there was a handwritten note from Rachel.

Dear Sarah,

Thank you so much for your submission. I found your story intriguing and thought-provoking. A real eye-opener, in fact. But I felt the ending was rather weak and so I regret we're unable to publish it. However, I like your style. I'd be very interested to see more of your work.

Gratefully yours,

Rachel Uttley

That's when I realised what I'd done. Like Oscar Wilde, I'd killed the thing I'd loved. And Rachel had made sure I knew it.

That's when my sleepless nights started.

And that's why I'm so very, very grateful for Roger and the case they call *Wagon Mound* (No.1). And for an understanding of proximity. Thanks to him, I've finally realised I'm not the guilty party here. Neither is Rachel.

The guilty party is the one who started the wagon rolling. Lovely, sexy, reckless Sam Uttley.

Breathtaking Ignorance

Every caterer's nightmare. The choking customer, collapsed on the floor gasping for breath. I'd already hurtled
through from the kitchen as soon as I heard the coughing
and spluttering, and I made it to his side just as he slumped
to the floor like a Bonfire Night guy, legs splayed, head
lolling, eyes popping.

The boardroom crowd were keeping their distance,
remembering all the strictures they'd ever heard about giving
people air. There was a nervous hush, the only sounds the
croaking gasps of the man on the floor. I knew exactly
who he was. Brian Bayliss, chief legal executive of Kaymen
Merchant Bank. I'd catered functions for him, both at the
bank's Canary Wharf headquarters and at his opulent house
in Suffolk, and I knew he was as pompous and bossy as they
come. But that didn't stop me kneeling down beside him and
dragging him into a sitting position so I could perform the
Heimlich manoeuvre. That's one of the many fascinating
things you learn at catering college. You encircle the victim
with your arms, hug them tightly and sharply, forcing the air
out of their lungs, which in turn frees whatever is blocking
their windpipe. The downside is that somebody usually ends
up covered in sick.

Bayliss was bright scarlet by now, his lips turning an
ominous blue. I got my arms round him, smelling the sweat
that mingled with his expensive cologne. I contracted my

arms, forcing his ribs inward. Nothing happened. His gasping sounded ever more frantic, less effective.

'I'll call an ambulance, Meg,' John Collings said desperately, moving towards the boardroom phone. He'd organised this lunch, and I could see this was the last contract for a directors' thrash that I'd be getting from him.

I tried the manoeuvre again. This time, Bayliss slumped heavily against me. The dreadful retching of his breathing suddenly ceased. The heaving in his chest seemed to have stopped. 'Oh my God,' I said. 'He's stopped breathing.'

A couple of the other guests moved forward and gingerly pulled Bayliss's still body away from me. I freed my skirt from under him and crawled round him on my knees, saying, 'Quick, the kiss of life.' Out of the corner of my eye I could see John slam the phone down. In the corner behind him, Tessa, the waitress who'd served him, was weeping quietly.

John's chief accountant had taken on the unenviable task of mouth-to-mouth resuscitation. Somehow, I knew he was wasting his time. I leaned back on my heels, muttering, 'I don't understand it. I just don't understand it.'

The ambulance crew arrived within five minutes and clamped an oxygen mask over his face. They strapped Bayliss to a stretcher and I followed them down the corridor and into the lift. David Bromley, Bayliss's deputy, climbed into the ambulance alongside me, looking like he wanted to ask what the hell I thought I was doing.

'It was my food he was eating,' I said defensively. 'I want to make sure he's all right.'

'Looks a bit late for that,' he said. He didn't sound filled with regret.

At the hospital, David and I found a quiet corner near the

WRVS coffee stall. I stared glumly at the floor and said softly, 'He didn't look like he was going to pull through.'

'No,' David agreed with a note almost of relish in his voice.

'You don't sound too upset,' I hazarded.

'That obvious, is it?' he asked pleasantly. 'No, I'm not upset. The bank will be a better place without him. The guy's a complete shit. He's a tyrant at the office and at home too, from what I can gather. He says jump and the only question you're allowed to ask is, how high? He goes through secretaries like other people go through rolls of Sellotape.'

'Oh God,' I groaned. 'So if he recovers, he'll probably sue me for negligence.'

'I doubt if he'd have a case. His own greed was too much of a contributory factor. I saw him stuffing down those chicken and garlic canapés like there was no tomorrow,' David consoled me.

Before we could say more, a weary-looking woman in a white coat approached us. 'Are you the two people who came in the ambulance with –', she checked her clipboard. 'Brian Bayliss?' We nodded. 'Are you related to Mr Bayliss?'

We shook our heads. 'I'm a colleague,' David said.

'And I catered the lunch where Mr Bayliss had his choking fit,' I revealed.

The doctor nodded. 'Can you tell me what Mr Bayliss had to eat?'

'Just some canapés. That's all we'd served by then,' I said defensively.

'And what exactly was in the canapés?'

'There were two sorts,' I explained. 'Smoked chicken or salmon and lobster.'

'Brian was eating the chicken ones,' David added helpfully. The doctor looked slightly puzzled. 'Are you sure?'

'Of course I'm sure. He never touched fish,' David added. 'He wouldn't even have it on the menu if we were hosting a function.'

'Look,' I said. 'What exactly is the problem here?'

The doctor sighed. 'Mr Bayliss has died, apparently as a result of anaphylactic shock.' We must both have looked bewildered, for she went on to explain. 'A profound allergic reaction. Essentially, the pathways in his respiratory tract just closed up. He couldn't physically get enough air into his lungs, so he asphyxiated. I've never heard of it being brought on by chicken, though. The most common cause is an allergic reaction to a bee sting,' she added thoughtfully.

'I know he was allergic to shellfish,' David offered. 'That's why he had this thing about never serving fish.'

'Oh my God,' I wailed. 'The lobster!' They both stared at me. 'I ground up the lobster shells into powder and mixed them with mayonnaise for the fish canapés. The mayo for the chicken ones had grilled red peppers and roast garlic mixed into it. They looked very similar. Surely there couldn't have been a mix-up in the kitchen?' I covered my face with my hands as I realised what had happened.

Of course, they both fussed over me and insisted it wasn't my fault. I pulled myself together after a few minutes, then the doctor asked David about Bayliss's next of kin. 'His wife's called Alexandra,' he told her, and recited their home number.

How did I know it was their home number? Not from catering executive lunches, I'm afraid. Perhaps I should have mentioned that Alexandra and I have been lovers for just over a year now. And that Brian was adamant that if she left him, he'd make sure she left without a penny from him. And, more importantly, that she'd never see her children again.

I just hope the mix-up with the mayo won't hurt my reputation for gourmet boardroom food too much.

White Nights, Black Magic

When night falls in St Petersburg, the dead become more palpable. In this city built on blood and bone, they're always present. But when darkness gathers, they're harder to escape. The frozen, drowned serfs who paid the price for Peter the Great's determination to fulfil Nostradamus's prediction that Venice would rise from the dead waters of the north; the assassinated tsars whose murders changed surprisingly little; the starved victims of the Wehrmacht's nine-hundred-day siege; the buried corpses of lords of the imagination such as Dostoevsky, Borodin and Rimsky-Korsakov – they're all there in the shifting shadows, their foetid breath tainting the chilly air that comes off the Neva and shivers through the streets.

My dead too. I never feel closer to Elinor than when I walk along the embankment of Vasilyevsky Ostrov on a winter's night. The familiar grandeur of the Hermitage and St Isaac's cathedral on the opposite bank touch me not at all. What resonates inside me is the sound of her voice, the touch of her hand, the spark of her eyes.

It shouldn't be this way. It shouldn't be the darkness that conjures her up for me, because we didn't make those memories in the dead core of winter. The love that exploded between us was a child of the light, a dream state that played itself out against the backdrop of the White Nights, those heady summer weeks when the sun never sets over St Petersburg.

Like all lovers, we thought the sun would never set on us either. But it did. And although Elinor isn't one of the St Petersburg dead, she comes back to haunt me when the city's ghosts drift through the streets in wraiths of river mist. I know too that this is no neutral visitation. Her presence demands something of me, and it's taken me a long time to figure out what that is. But I know now. Elinor understood that Russia can be a cruel and terrible place, and also that I am profoundly Russian. So tonight, I will make reparation.

Three summers ago, Elinor unpacked her bags in the Moscow Hotel down at the far end of Nevsky Prospekt. She'd never been to Russia before, and when we met that first evening, she radiated a buzz of excitement that enchanted me. We Russians are bound to our native land by a terrible, doomed sentimental attachment, and we are predisposed to like anyone who shows the slightest sign of sharing that love.

But there was more than that linking us from the very beginning. Anyone who has ever been in an abusive relationship has had their mental map altered forever. It's hard to explain precisely how that manifests itself, but once you've been there, you recognise it in another. An almost imperceptible flicker in the eyes; some tiny shift in the body language; an odd moment of deference in the dialogue. Whatever the signals, they're subconsciously registered by those of us who are members of the same club. In that very first encounter, I read that kinship between myself and Elinor.

By the time I met Elinor, I was well clear of the marriage that had thrown me off balance, turned me from a confident, assured professional woman into a bundle of insecurities. I was back on even keel, in control of my own destiny and certain I would never walk into that nightmare again. I wasn't so sure about Elinor.

She seemed poised and assertive. She was a well-qualified doctor who had gained a reputation for her work on addiction with intravenous drug users in her native Manchester. She was the obvious choice for a month-long exchange visit to share her experiences with local medical professionals and voluntary-sector workers struggling to come to terms with the heroin epidemic sweeping St Petersburg. She exuded a quiet competence and an easy manner. But still, I recognised the secret shame, the hidden scars.

I had been chosen to act as her interpreter because I'd spent two years of my post-graduate medical training in San Francisco. I was nervous about the assignment because I had no formal training in interpreting, but my boss made it clear there was no room for argument. The budget wouldn't run to a qualified interpreter, and besides, I knew all the technical terminology. I explained this to Elinor over a glass of wine in the half-empty bar after the official dinner with the meeting-and-greeting party.

Some specialists might have regarded my confession as a slight on their importance. But Elinor just grinned and said, 'Natasha, you're a doctor, you can probably make me sound much more sensible than I can manage myself. Now, if you're not rushing off, maybe you can show me round a little, help me get my bearings?'

We walked out of the hotel, round the corner to the Metro station. Her eyes were wide, absorbed by everything. The amputee war veterans round the kiosks; the endless escalator; the young woman slumped against the door of the train carriage, vodka bottle dangling from her fingers, wrecked mascara in snail trails down her cheeks; Elinor drank it all in, tossing occasional questions at me.

We emerged back into daylight at the opposite end of Nevsky Prospekt, and I steered her round the big tourist sights. The cathedral, the Admiralty, the Hermitage, then back along the embankment to the Fontanka Canal. Because she was still operating on UK time, she didn't really register the White Nights phenomenon at first. It was only when I pointed out that it was already eleven o'clock and she probably needed to think about getting some sleep that she realised her normal cues for waking and sleeping were going to be absent for the next four weeks.

'How do you cope with the constant light?' she said, waving an arm at a sky only a couple of shades lighter than her eyes.

I shrugged. 'I pull the pillow over my head. But your hotel will have heavy curtains, I think.' I flagged down a passing Lada and asked the driver to take us back to the hotel.

'It's all so alien,' she said softly.

'It'll get worse before it gets better,' I told her. I dropped her at the hotel and kept the car on. As the driver weaved through the potholed streets back to my apartment on Vasilyevsky Ostrov, I couldn't escape the image of her wide-eyed wondering face.

But then, I wasn't exactly trying.

Over the next week, I spent most of my waking hours with Elinor. Mostly it was work, constantly stretching my brain to keep pace with the exchange of information that flowed back and forth between Elinor and my colleagues. But in the evenings, we fell into the habit of eating together, then strolling round the city so she could soak up the atmosphere. I didn't mind. There were plenty of other things I could have been doing, but my friends would still be there after she left town. What I wasn't allowing myself to acknowledge was that I was falling in love with her.

On the sixth night, she finally started opening up. 'You know I mentioned my partner?' she said, filling our wine glasses to avoid my eyes.

'He's a lawyer, right?' I said.

Her mouth twisted up at one corner. 'He's a she.' She flicked a quick glance at me. 'Does that surprise you?'

I couldn't keep the smile from my face. For days, I'd been telling myself off for wishful thinking, but I'd been right. 'It takes one to know one,' I said.

'You're gay?' Elinor sounded startled.

'Labels are for medicines,' I said. 'But lately, I seem to have given up on men.'

'You have a girlfriend?' Now, her eyes were on mine. I didn't know what to read into their level stare, which unsettled me a little.

'Nothing serious,' I said. 'A friend I sleep with from time to time, when she's in town. Just fun, for both of us. Not like you.'

She looked away again. 'No. Not like me.'

Something about the angle of her head, the downcast eyes and the hand that gripped the wine glass told me my first instinct had been right. Whatever she might say next, I knew that this apparently confident woman was in thrall to someone who stripped her of her self-esteem. 'Tell me about her,' I said.

'Her name's Claire. She's a lawyer, specialising in intellectual property. She's very good. We've been together ten years. She's very smart, very strong, very beautiful. She keeps my feet on the ground.'

I wanted to tell her that love should be about flying, not about the force of gravity. But I didn't. 'Do you miss her?'

Again, she met my eyes. 'I thought I would. But I've been so busy.' She smiled. 'And you're such good company, you've kept me from being lonely.'

'It's been my pleasure. Where would you like to go this evening?'

Her gaze was level, unblinking. 'I'd like to see where you live.'

I tried to stay cool. 'It's not very impressive.'

'You don't have to impress me. I'd just like to see a real Russian home. I'm fed up with hotels and restaurants.'

So we took the Metro to Vasileostrovskaya and walked down Sredny Prospekt to the Tenth Line, where I live in a two-roomed apartment on the second floor. Buying it took every penny I managed to save in the US, and it's pretty drab by Western standards, but to a Russian it feels like total luxury to have so much space to oneself. I showed Elinor into the living room with some nervousness. I'd never brought a Westerner home before.

She looked round the white walls with their Chagall posters and the second-hand furniture covered with patchwork throws, then turned to me and smiled. 'I like it,' she said.

I turned away, feeling embarrassed. 'Interior design hasn't really hit Russia,' I said. 'Would you like a drink? I've got tea or coffee or vodka.'

'Vodka, please.'

There is a moment that comes with drinking vodka Russian style when inhibitions slip away. That's the time to stop drinking, before you get too drunk to do anything with the window of opportunity. I knew Elinor had hit the moment when she leaned into me and said, 'I really love this country.'

I pushed her dark hair away from her forehead and said, 'Russia can be a very cruel place. We Russians are dangerous.'

'You don't feel very dangerous to me,' she whispered, her breath hot against my neck.

'I'm Russian. I'm trouble. The two go together like hand in glove.'

'Mmm. I like the sound of that. Your hand, my glove.'

'That would be very dangerous.'

She chuckled softly. 'I feel the need for a little danger, Natasha.'

And so we made trouble.

Of course, she went back to England. She didn't want to, but she had no choice. Her visa was about to expire, she had work commitments at home. And there was Claire. She had said very little about her lover, but I understood how deeply ingrained was her subservience. The clues were there, both sexually and emotionally. Claire wasn't physically violent, but emotional abuse can cause damage that is far more profound. Elinor had learned the lesson of submission so thoroughly it was entrenched in her soul. No matter how deep the love that had sprung up between us, in her heart she couldn't escape the conviction that she belonged to Claire.

It didn't stop us loving each other. We e-mailed daily,

sometimes several times a day. We managed to speak on the phone every two or three weeks, sometimes for an hour at a time. A couple of months after she'd gone back, she called in distress. Claire had accepted a new job in London, and was insisting Elinor abandon her work in Manchester and move to the capital with her. I gently suggested this might be the opportunity for Elinor to free herself, not necessarily for me but for her own sake. But I knew even as I spoke it was pointless. Until Claire decided it was over, Elinor had no other option but to stay. I understood that; I had only managed to free myself when my husband had grown tired of me. I wanted to save her, but I didn't know how.

Three months later, they'd moved. Elinor had found a job at one of the London teaching hospitals. She didn't have the same degree of autonomy she'd enjoyed in Manchester, and she found it much less challenging. But at least she was able to use some of her expertise, and she liked the team she was working with.

I was actually reading one of her e-mails when my boss called me into his office. 'You know I'm supposed to go to London next week? The conference on HIV and intravenous drug use?'

I nodded. Lucky bastard, I'd thought when the invitation came through. 'I remember.'

'My wife has been diagnosed with breast cancer,' he said abruptly. 'They're operating on Monday. So you'll have to go instead.'

It was an uncomfortable way to achieve my heart's desire, but there was nothing I could do about my boss's misfortune. A few days later, I was walking through customs and immigration and into Elinor's arms. We went straight to my hotel and dived back into the dangerous waters. Hand in glove. Moths to a flame.

Four days of the conference. Three evenings supposedly socialising with colleagues, but in reality, time we could steal to be together. Except that on the last night, the plans went spectacularly awry. Instead of a discreet knock at my bedroom door, the phone rang. Elinor's voice was unnaturally bright. 'Hi, Natasha,' she said. 'I'm down in reception. I hope you don't mind, but I've brought Claire with me. She wanted to meet you.'

Panic choked me like a gloved hand. 'I'll be right down,' I managed to say. I dressed hurriedly, fingers fumbling zip and buttons, mouth muttering Russian curses. What was Claire up to? Was this simply about control, or was there more to it? Had she sussed what was going on between Elinor and me? With dry mouth and damp palms, I rode the lift to the ground floor, trying to hold it together. Not for myself, but for Elinor's sake.

They looked good together. Elinor's sable hair, denim blue eyes and olive skin on one side of the table, a contrast to Claire's blonde hair and surprising brown eyes. Where Elinor's features were small and neat, Claire's were strong and well-defined. She looked like someone you'd rather have on your side than against you. While Elinor looked nervous, her fingers picking at a cocktail coaster, Claire leaned back in her seat, a woman in command of her surroundings.

As I approached, feeling hopelessly provincial next to their urban chic, Claire was first to her feet. 'You must be Natasha,' she said, her smile lighting her eyes. 'I'm so pleased to meet you.' I extended a hand, but her hand was on my shoulder as she leaned in to kiss me on both cheeks. 'I've been telling

Elinor off for keeping you to herself. I do hope you don't mind me butting in, but I so wanted to meet you.'

Control, then, I thought, daring to let myself feel relieved as I sat down at the table. At once, Claire stamped her authority on the conversation. How was I enjoying London? Was it as I expected? How were things in Russia? How was life changing for ordinary people?

By the time we hit the second drink, she was flirting with me. She wanted to prove she could own me the way she owned her lover. Elinor was consigned to the sidelines, and her acquiescence to this confirmed all I believed about their relationship. My heart ached for her, an uneasy mixture of love and pity making me feel faintly queasy. I don't know how I managed to eat dinner with them. All I wanted was to steal Elinor away, to prove to her she had the power to take her life back and make of it what she wanted.

But of course, she left with Claire. And in the morning, I was on a plane back to St Petersburg, half-convinced that the only healthy thing for me to do was to end our relationship.

I didn't. I couldn't. In spite of everything I know about the tentacles of emotional abuse, I found it impossible to reject the notion that I might somehow be Elinor's saviour. So I kept on writing, kept on telling her how much I loved her when she called, kept on seeing her face in my mind's eye whenever I slept with other people.

More weeks trickled by, then out of the blue, an e-mail in a very different tone arrived.

> Natasha, darling. Can you get to Brussels next weekend? I need to see you. I can arrange air tickets if you can arrange

a visa. Please, if it's humanly possible, come to Brussels. I love you. E.

I tried to get her to tell me what was going on, but she refused. All I could do was fix up a visa and collect the tickets from the travel agent. When Elinor opened the hotel room door, she looked a dozen years older than when I'd seen her in London. My first thought was that Claire had discovered our affair. But the truth was infinitely worse.

We'd barely hugged when Elinor was moving away from me. She curled up in the room's only armchair and covered her face with her hands. 'I'm so scared,' she said.

I crouched down beside her and gently pulled her hands away from her face. 'What's wrong, Elinor?'

She flicked her tongue along dry lips. 'You know I'm mostly working with HIV patients now?'

It wasn't what I'd expected to hear, but somehow I already knew what was coming. 'Yes, I know.'

A deep, shuddering breath. 'A few weeks ago, I got a needle stick.' Her eyes filled with tears. 'Natasha, I'm HIV positive.'

Intellectually, I knew this wasn't a death sentence. So did Elinor. But in that instant, it felt like the end of the world. I couldn't think of anything else that would assert her right to a future, so I cradled her in my arms and said, 'Let's make love.'

At first, she resisted. But we both knew too much about the transmission routes of the virus for the idea of putting me at risk to take deep root. Sure, it meant changes for how we made love, but that was a tiny price to pay for the affirmation that her life would go on.

We spent the weekend behind closed doors, loving each other, talking endlessly about what she'd have to do to maximise her chances of long-term health. At some point on Sunday, she confessed that Claire had refused to have sex since the diagnosis. That made me angrier than anything I'd previously known or suspected about the abuse of power between the two of them.

That parting was the worst. I wanted to take her home with me. I wanted our passion to be her cocoon against the virus. But realistically, even if she'd been able to leave Claire, we both knew her best chance for access to the latest treatments would be to remain in the West.

Oddly, in spite of the cataclysmic nature of her news, nothing really changed between us. The old channels of communication remained intact, the intensity between us diminished not at all. The only difference was that now we also discussed drug treatments, dietary regimes and alternative therapies.

Then one Monday, silence. No e-mail. I wasn't too worried. There had been days when Elinor hadn't been able to write, but mostly those had been on the weekend when she'd not been able to escape Claire's oppressive attention. Tuesday dragged past, then Wednesday. No reply to my e-mails, no phone call. Nothing. Finally, on the Thursday, I tried to call her at work.

Voice-mail. I left an innocuous message and hung up. Friday brought more silence. The weekend was a nightmare. I checked my e-mail neurotically, every hour, on the hour. I was afraid to go out in case she called, and by Sunday night my apartment felt like a prison cell. Monday, I spoke to her voice-mail again. Desperation had me in its grip. I even considered taking the chance of calling her at home. Instead, I hit on the idea of calling the department secretary.

'I've been trying to contact Dr Stevenson,' I said when I finally got through.

'Dr Stevenson is away at present,' the stiff English voice said.

'When will she be back?'

'I really can't say.'

I'd been fighting fear for days, but now my defences were crumbling fast. 'Look, I'm a personal friend of Elinor's,' I said. 'From St Petersburg. I'm due to be in London this week and we were supposed to meet. But I've had no reply to my e-mails, and I really need to contact her about our arrangements. Can you help me?'

The voice softened. 'I'm afraid Dr Stevenson's very ill. She won't be well enough to have a meeting this week.'

'Is she in hospital?' Somehow, I managed to keep hold of my English in the teeth of the terror that was ripping through me.

'Yes. She's a patient here.'

'Can you put me through to the ward she's on?'

'I'm . . . I'm sorry, she's in intensive care. She won't be able to speak to you.'

I don't remember ending the call. Just the desperate pain her words brought in their wake. I couldn't make sense of what I was hearing. It ran counter to all I knew about HIV and AIDS. It was a matter of months since Elinor had been infected. For her to be so ill so soon was virtually unheard of. People lived with HIV for years. Some people lived with AIDS for years. It was impossible.

But the impossible had happened.

* * *

I spent the next couple of days in a frenzy of activity, staving off my alarm with action. I couldn't afford the flight, but I managed to get the money together by borrowing from my three closest friends. I couldn't explain to my boss why I needed the time off and we were under pressure at work, so there was no prospect of making it to London before the weekend. The rest of my spare time I spent trying to sort out a visa.

By Thursday evening, I was almost organised. The travel agent had sworn she would call first thing in the morning about last-minute flights. I'd managed to persuade a colleague to cover for me at the beginning of the following week so I had a couple of extra days in hand. And the visa was promised for the next afternoon.

I'd just walked through the door of my apartment when the phone rang. I ran across the room and grabbed it. '*Da?*'

Breathing rasped in my ear. 'Natasha.' Elinor's voice was little more than a whisper but there was no mistaking it.

'Elinor.' I couldn't speak through the lump in my throat.

'I'm dying, Nat. Pneumocystis. Drug-resistant strain.' She could only speak on the exhalation of her shallow breaths. 'Wanted to call you. Brain's fucked, couldn't remember the number. Claire wouldn't . . . bring me my organiser. Had to get nurse to get it from my office.'

'Never mind. We're talking now. Elinor, I'm coming over. At the weekend.'

'No. Don't come, Nat. Please. I love you too much. Don't want you to remember . . . this. Remember the good stuff.'

'I want to see you.' Tears running down my face, I struggled to keep them out of my voice.

'Please, no. Nat, I wanted you to know . . . loving you?

Best thing that ever hit me. Wanted to say goodbye. Wanted to say, be happy.'

'*Ya tebyeh lublu*,' I gulped. 'Don't die on me, Elinor.'

'Wish I had . . . choice. Trouble with being a doctor . . . you know what's happening to you. A couple of days, Nat. Then it's . . . DNR time. I love you.'

'I know.'

The breathing stopped and another voice came on the line. 'Hello? I'm sorry, Dr Stevenson is too tired to talk any more.'

'How bad is it?' I don't know how I managed to speak without choking.

'I shouldn't really speak to anyone who isn't immediate family,' she hedged.

'Please. You saw how important this call was to her. I'm a doctor too, I know the score.'

'I'm afraid her condition is very serious. She's not responding to treatment. It's likely we'll have to put her on a ventilator very soon.'

'It's true she's signed a DNR?'

'I'm very sorry,' the nurse said after a short pause.

'Take good care of her.' I replaced the phone as gently as if it had been Elinor's hand. I'd spent enough time in hospitals to read between the lines. Elinor hadn't been mistaken. She was dying.

I never went to London. It would have been an act of selfishness. Claire never called me, which told me that she knew the truth. But the nurse from intensive care did phone, on the Sunday morning at nine twenty-seven a.m. Elinor had asked her to let me know when she died. A couple of weeks later, I wrote to Claire, saying I'd heard about Elinor's death from a colleague and expressing my sympathy. I'm not sure why I did, but sometimes our subconscious paves the way for our future actions without bothering to inform us.

Grief twisted in me like a rusty knife for a long time. But everything transmutes eventually, and slowly it turned to anger. Generally when people die, there's nobody to blame. But Elinor's death wasn't like that. The responsibility for what happened to her lay with Claire, impossible to dodge.

If Claire had not ruled her with fear, Elinor would have left her for me. If Claire had not stripped her of her self-confidence, Elinor would have stayed in Manchester and someone else would have suffered that needle stick. However you cut it, Elinor would still be alive if Claire had not made her feel like a possession.

For a long time, my anger felt pointless, a dry fire burning inside me that consumed nothing. Then out of the blue, I had an e-mail from Claire.

> Hello, Natasha. I'm sorry I never got in touch with you after Elinor's death, but as you will imagine, it was not an easy time for me. However, I am attending a conference in St Petersburg next month, and I wondered if you would like to meet up for dinner. I have such fond memories of the evening we spent together in London. It might bring us both some solace to spend some time together. Let me know if this would suit you. Best wishes, Claire Somerville.

The arrangements are made. Tonight, she will come to my apartment for dinner. I know she will seduce me. She won't be able to resist the challenge of possessing the woman

Elinor loved.

But Claire is a Russian virgin. She doesn't understand the first thing about us. She will have no sense of the cruelty or the danger that always lurks beneath the surface, particularly in this city of the dead.

She will not suspect the narcotic in the alcohol. And when she wakes, she won't notice the scab on the vein in the back of her knee. The syringe is loaded already, thick with virus, carefully maintained in perfect culture conditions.

It's almost certain she'll have longer than Elinor. But sooner or later, the black magic of those White Nights will take its revenge. And perhaps then, my dead will sleep.

The Writing on the Wall

I've never written anything on a toilet wall before, but I don't know what else to do. Please help me. My boyfriend is violent towards me. He hits me and I don't know where to turn.

Kick the bastard where it hurts. Give him a taste of his own medicine.

Get out of the relationship now before he does you serious injury. Battering men only batter with our consent.

I can't believe these responses. I asked for help, not a lecture. I love him, don't you realise that? He was raped and battered as a child. Are we just supposed to ignore damaged people?

If you don't get out of the relationship, then you're going to end up another one of the damaged people. And who will help you then?

Ask your friends for their support in dealing with him. When his violence begins, leave the house and go and stay with a friend.

I can't walk out on him. He needs me. And I can't tell my friends because I'm too ashamed to admit to them that I'm in a relationship with a man who batters me.

Sooner or later they're going to notice and then they're going to feel angry that you've excluded them from something so important.

How come you're the one who's ashamed, not him? He's the one dishing out the violence, after all.

Like I said at the start, fight back. Let him know what being hurt feels like.

He knows what being hurt feels like. He spent his childhood being hurt. And he is ashamed of his violence. He hates himself for his behaviour, and he's always really sorry afterwards.

Well, whoopee shit! That must really help your bruises!

This is the first time I've been in this loo and I can't believe how unsupportive you're all being to this woman! Sister, there is counselling available. You deserve help; there's a number for the confidential helpline in the student handbook. Use it, please.

It's not just you that needs counselling. Tell your boyfriend that unless he comes for counselling with you, you will leave him. If he refuses, then you know his apologies aren't worth a toss.

Leave him; tell him you'll only take him back once he has had counselling and learned to deal with his problem in a way that doesn't include violence. Anything else is a betrayal of all the other women who get battered every day.

Thanks for the suggestion. I've phoned the helpline and we're both going to meet the counsellor next week.

I still say leave him till he's got himself sorted out. He's only going to end up resenting you for making him go through all this shit.

I'm glad you've taken this step forward; let us know how you go on.

Sorry it's taken me so long to get back to you all. My lectures were moved out of this building for a couple of weeks because of the ceiling collapse. We've had three joint counselling sessions so far and I really feel that things are getting better!

You mean he only batters you once a week instead of every night?

Now he's made the first step, you can tell him you're going to move out till the course of counselling has finished. You owe it to yourself and to the other victimised women out there to show this batterer that he is no longer in a position of power over you.

Well done. Good luck.

I'm not moving out on him. I'm going to stick with him because he's trying so hard. He's really making the effort to deal with his anger and to resolve the conflicts that make him lash out at me. I love him, everybody seems to keep forgetting that. If you love somebody, you want to help them get better, not abandon them because they're not perfect.

Answer the question; is he still hitting you?

Oh for God's sake, leave her alone. Can't you see she's having enough of a struggle helping the guy she loves without having the holier-than-thou tendency on her back?

Save us from the bleeding hearts. If he's still hitting her, she's still collaborating with his oppressive behaviour. She should walk away while she can still walk.

So where's she supposed to go? A woman's refuge packed with damaged kids and mothers isn't exactly the ideal place to study, is it?

Anywhere's got to be better than a place where you get hurt constantly.

And you think battering someone is the only way to hurt them? Grow up!

He hasn't hit me for over a week now. He's made a real breakthrough. He has contacted his mother for the first time in three years and confronted her with the abuse he experienced from his stepfather. He says he feels like he's released so much pressure just by telling her about it.

Surprise, surprise. Now he's found a woman to blame, he's going to be all right.

Yeah, how come he hasn't confronted the abuser? How come he has to offload his guilt on his poor bloody mother who was probably battered too?

Leave him. You are perpetuating the circle of violence. He will see your forgiveness as condoning his behaviour. Break out. Now. If you stay, you are as bad as he is.

Don't listen to them. Stick with him. You are making progress. People can change.

Bollocks. Been there, done that, got the bruises. Men who abuse do it because they like it, not because of some behaviour pattern they can change as easily as giving up smoking. The only way to stop being the victim of abuse is to walk away.

He is making changes. I know he is. It's not easy for him and sometimes it feels like he hates me because I'm the one who persuaded him to confront his problems, he's started to get really jealous and suspicious, even following me to lectures sometimes. He's convinced that because I suggested the counselling, I'm seeing some women's group that is trying to talk me into leaving him. If he only knew the truth! Are there any women out there who have been through this, who would be prepared to do some one-to-one counselling with me?

Ah, the power of the sisterhood of the toilet wall! He's right, though, isn't he? We are trying to make you see sense and get out of this destructive relationship.

Sounds like you're swapping one problem for another. The guy is major-league bad news. Sometimes if you love people, the best thing you can do for them is to leave them.

I know what you're going through. I'll meet you on Saturday morning on the Kelvin walkway under the Queen Margaret Drive bridge at ten thirty. Come alone. Make sure he's not with you. I'll be watching. If you can't make this Saturday, I'll be there every week until you can.

From the *Scottish Sunday Dispatch*:

BODY FOUND IN RIVER KELVIN

Police launched a murder hunt last night after the battered body of a woman student was found floating in the River Kelvin.

A woman walking her dog on the river walkway near Kelvinbrige spotted the body tangled in the roots of a tree.

Police revealed that the victim, who was fully dressed, had been beaten about the head before being thrown in the river.

The woman, whose name is not being released until her family can be contacted, was a second-year biochemistry student at Glasgow University.

Police are appealing for witnesses who may have seen the woman and her attacker on the Kelvin walkway upstream of Kelvinbridge yesterday.

A spokeswoman for the Students' Union said last night, 'This is a terrible tragedy. When a woman gets killed in broad daylight in a public place, you start wondering if there is anywhere that is safe for us to be.'

Keeping on the Right Side of the Law

Just imagine trying to get a straight job when you've been a villain all your life. Even supposing I could bullshit my way round an application form, how the fuck do I blag my way through an interview, when the only experience I've got of interviews, I've always had a brief sitting next to me reminding the thickhead dickheads on the other side of the table that I'm not obliged to answer? I mean, it's not a technique that's going to score points with the personnel manager, is it?

You can imagine it, can't you? 'Mr Finnieston, your application form was a little vague as to dates. Can you give us a more accurate picture of your career structure to date?'

Well, yeah. I started out with burglary when I was eight. My two older brothers figured I was little enough to get in toilet windows, so they taught me how to hold the glass firm with rubber suckers then cut round the edge with a glass cutter. I'd take out the window and pass it down to them, slide in through the gap and open the back door for them. Then they'd clean out the telly, the video and the stereo while I kept watch out the back.

All good things have to come to an end, though, and by the time I was eleven, I'd got too big for the toilet windows, and besides, I wanted a bigger cut than those greedy thieving bastards would give me. That's when I started doing cars. They called me Sparky on account of I'd go out with a spark plug tied on to a piece of cord. You whirl the plug around like a cowboy with a lasso, and when it's going fast enough, you just flick the wrist and bingo, the driver's window shatters like one of them fake windows they use in the films. Hardly makes a sound.

Inside a minute and I'd have the stereo out. I sold them round the pubs for a fiver a time. In a good night, I could earn a fifty, just like that, no hassle.

But I've always been ambitious, and that was my downfall. One of my mates showed me how to hot-wire the ignition so I could have it away on my toes with the car as well as the sounds. By then, one of my brothers was doing a bit of work for a bloke who had a second-hand car pitch down Strangeways and a quiet little back-street garage where his team ringed stolen cars and turned them out with a whole new identity to sell on to mug punters who knew no better.

Only, he wasn't as clever as he thought he was, and one night I rolled up with a Ford Escort and drove right into the middle of a raid. It was wall-to-wall Old Bill that night, and I ended up in a different part of Strangeways, behind bars. Of course, I was too young to do proper time, and my brief got me out of there and into a juvenile detention centre faster than you could say 'of previous good character'.

It's true, what they say about the nick. You do learn how to be a better criminal, just so long as you do what it tells you in all them American self-help books in the prison library. You want to be successful, then hang out with successful people and do what they do. Only, of course, anybody who's banged up is, by definition, not half as fucking successful as they should be.

Anyway, I watched and listened and learned and I made some good mates that first time inside. And when I came out, I was ready for bigger and better things. Back then, banks and Post Offices were still a nice little earner. They hadn't learned about shatterproof glass and grilles and all that bollocks. You just ran in, waved a shooter around, jumped the counter and cleaned the place out. You could be in and out in five minutes, with enough in your sports bag to see you clear for the next few months.

I loved it.

It was a clean way to earn a living. Well, mostly it was. OK, a couple of times we ran into one of them have-a-go heroes. You'd think it was their money, honest to God you would. Now, I've always believed you should be able to do a job, in and out, and nobody gets hurt. But if some dickhead is standing between me and the out, and it's me or him, I'm not going to stand there and ask him politely to move aside, am I? No, fuck it, you've got to show him who's in charge. One shot into the ceiling, and if he's still standing there, well, it's his own fault, isn't it? You've got to be professional, haven't you? You've got to show you mean business.

And I must have been good at it, because I only ever got a tug the once, and they couldn't pin a thing on me. Yeah, OK, I did end up doing a three stretch around about then, but that was for what you might call extra-curricular activities. When I found out Johnny the Hat was giving one to my brother's wife, well, I had to make an example of him, didn't I? I mean, family's family. She might be a slag and a dog, but anybody that thinks they can fuck with my family is going to find out different. You'd think Johnny would have had the sense not to tell the Dibble who put him in the hospital, but some people haven't got the brains they were born with. They had him in witness protection before the trial, but of course all that ended after I went down. And when I was getting through my three with visits from the family, I had the satisfaction of knowing that Johnny's family were visiting his grave. Like I say, families have got to stick together.

By the time I got out, things had changed. The banks and building societies had wised up and sharpened up their act and the only people trying to rob them were amateurs and fucking eejits.

Luckily, I'd met Tommy inside. Honest to God, it was like it was written in the fucking stars. I knew all about robbing and burgling, and Tommy knew all there was to know about antiques. What he also knew was that half the museums and stately homes of England – not to mention our neighbours in Europe – had alarm systems that were an embarrassment.

I put together a dream team, and Tommy set up the fencing operation, and we were in business. We raped so many private collections I lost count. The MO was simple. We'd spend the summer on research trips. We'd case each place once. Then we'd go back three weeks later to case it again, leaving enough time for the security vids to be wiped of our previous visit. We'd figure out the weak points and draw up the plans. Then we'd wait till the winter, when most of them were closed up for the season, with nothing more than a skeleton staff.

We'd pick a cold, wet, miserable night, preferably with a bit of wind. That way, any noise we made got swallowed up in the weather. Then we'd go in, seven-pound sledges straight through the vulnerable door or window, straight to the cabinets that held the stuff we'd identified as worth nicking. Here's a tip, by the way. Even if they've got toughened glass in the cases, chances are it's still only got a wooden frame. Smack that on the corner with a three-pound club hammer and the whole thing falls to bits and you're in.

Mostly, we were off the estate and miles away before the local bizzies even rolled up. Nobody ever got hurt, except in the pocket.

They were the best years of my life. Better than sex, that moment when you're in, you do the business and you're out again. The rush is purer than you'll ever get from any drug. Not that I know about that from personal experience, because I've never done drugs and I never will. I hate drug dealers more than I hate coppers. I've removed my fair share of them from my patch over the years. Now they know not to come peddling their shit on my streets. But a couple of the guys I work with, they like their Charlie or whizz when they're not working, and they swear that they've never had a high like they get when they're doing the business.

We did some crackers. A museum in France where they'd spent two million quid on their state-of-the-art security system. They had a grand opening do where they were shouting their mouths off about how their museum was burglar-proof. We did it that very night. We rigged up pulleys from the building across the street, wound ourselves across like we were the SAS and went straight in through the skylight. They said we got away with stuff worth half a million quid. Not that we made anything like that off it. I think I cleared fifteen-K that night, after expenses. Still, who dares wins, eh?

We only ever took stuff we already knew we had a market for. Well, mostly. One time, I fell in love with this Rembrandt. I just loved that picture. It was a self-portrait, and just looking at it, you knew the geezer like he was one of your mates. It was hanging on this Duke's wall, right next to the cases of silver we'd earmarked. On the night, on the spur of the moment, I lifted the Rembrandt an' all.

Tommy went fucking ape. He said we'd never shift that, that we'd never find a buyer. I told him I didn't give a shit, it wasn't for sale anyway. He thought I'd completely lost the plot when I said I was taking it home.

I had it on the bedroom wall for six months. But it wasn't right. A council house in Wythenshawe just doesn't go with a Rembrandt. So one night, I wrapped it up in a tarpaulin and left it in a field next to the Duke's gaff. I rang the local radio station phone-in from a call box and told them where they could find the Rembrandt. I hated giving it up, mind you, and I wouldn't have done if I'd have had a nicer house.

But that's not the sort of tale you can tell a personnel manager, is it?

'And why are you seeking a change of employment, Mr Finnieston?'

Well, it's down to Kim, innit?

I've known Kimmy since we were at school together. She was a looker then, and time hasn't taken that away from her. I always fancied her, but never got round to asking her out. By the time I was back in circulation after my first stretch, she'd taken up with Danny McGann, and before I worked up the bottle to make a move, bingo, they were married.

I ran into her again about a year ago. She was on a girls' night out in Rothwell's, a gaggle of daft women acting like they were still teenagers. Just seeing her made me feel like a teenager an' all. I sent a bottle of champagne over to their table, and of course Kimmy came over to thank me for it. She always had good manners.

Any road, it turned out her and Danny weren't exactly happy families any more. He was working away a lot, leaving her with the two girls, which wasn't exactly a piece of cake. Mind you, she's done well for herself. She's got a really good job, managing a travel agency. A lot of responsibility and a lot of respect from her bosses. We started seeing each other, and I felt like I'd come up on the lottery.

The only drawback is that after a few months, she tells me she can't be doing with the villainy. She's got a proposition for me. If I go straight, she'll kick Danny into touch and move in with me.

So that's why I'm trying to figure out a way to make an honest living. You can see that convincing a bunch of suits they should give me a job would be difficult. 'Thank you very much, Mr Finnieston, but I'm afraid you don't quite fit our present requirements.'

The only way anybody's ever going to give me a job is if I monster them into it, and somehow I don't think the straight world works like that. You can't go around personnel offices saying, 'I know where you live. So gizza job or the Labrador gets it.'

This is where I'm up to when I meet my mate Chrissie for a drink. You wouldn't think it to look at her, but Chrissie writes them hard-as-nails cop dramas for the telly. She looks more like one of them bleeding-heart social workers, with her wholemeal jumpers and jeans. But Chrissie's dead sound, her and her girlfriend both. The girlfriend's a brief, but in spite of that, she's straight. That's probably because she doesn't do criminal stuff, just divorces and child custody and all that bollocks.

So I'm having a pint with Chrissie in one of them trendy

bars in Chorlton, all wooden floors and hard chairs and fifty different beers, none of them ones you've ever heard of except Guinness. And I'm telling her about my little problem. Halfway down the second pint, she gets that look in her eyes, the dreamy one that tells me something I've said has set the wheels in motion inside her head. Usually, I see the results six months later on the telly. I love that. Sitting down with Kimmy and going, 'See that? I told Chrissie about that scam. Course, she's softened it up a bit, but it's my tale.'

'I've got an idea,' Chrissie says.

'What? You're going to write a series about some poor fucker trying to go straight?' I say.

'No, a job. Well, sort of a job.' She knocks back the rest of her pint and grabs her coat. 'Leave it with me. I'll get back to you. Stay lucky.' And she's off, leaving me surrounded by the well-meaning like the last covered wagon hemmed in by the Apaches.

A week goes by, with me trying to talk my way into setting up a little business doing one-day hall sales. But everybody I approach thinks I'm up to something. They can't believe I want to do anything the straight way, so all I get offered is fifty kinds of bent gear. I am sick as a pig by the time I get the call from Chrissie.

This time, we meet round her house. Me, Chrissie and the girlfriend, Sarah the solicitor. We settled down with our bottles of Belgian pop and Sarah kicks off. 'How would you like to work on a freelance basis for a consortium of solicitors?' she asks.

I can't help myself. I just burst out laughing. 'Do what?' I go.

'Just hear me out. I spend a lot of my time dealing with women who are being screwed over by the men in their life. Some of them have been battered, some of them have been emotionally abused, some of them are being harassed by their exes. Sometimes, it's just that they're trying to get a square deal for themselves and their kids, only the bloke knows how to play the system and they end up with nothing while he laughs all the way to the bank. For most of these women, the law either can't sort it out or it won't. I even had a case where two coppers called to a domestic gave evidence in court against the woman, saying she was completely out of control and irrational and all the bloke was doing was exerting reasonable force to protect himself.'

'Bastards,' I say. 'So what's this got to do with me?'

'People doing my job get really frustrated,' Sarah says. 'There's a bunch of us get together for a drink now and again, and we've been talking for a long time about how we've stopped believing the law has all the answers. Most of these blokes are bullies and cowards. Their women wouldn't see them for dust if they had anybody to stand up for them. So what we're proposing is that we'd pay you to sort these bastards out.'

I can't believe what I'm hearing. A brief offering me readies to go round and heavy the kind of toerags I'd gladly sort out as a favour? There has to be a catch. 'You're not telling me the Legal Aid would pay for that, are you?' I say.

Sarah grins. 'Behave, Terry. I'm talking a strictly unofficial arrangement. I thought you could go and explain the error of their ways to these blokes. Introduce them to your base-ball bat. Tell them if they don't behave, you'll be visiting them again in a less friendly mode. Tell them that they'll be getting a bill for incidental legal expenses incurred on their partners' behalf and if they don't come up with the cash pronto monto, you'll be coming round to make a collection. I'm sure they'll respond very positively to your approaches.'

'You want me to go round and teach them a lesson?' I'm still convinced this is a wind-up.

'That's about the size of it.'

'And you'll pay me?'

'We thought a basic rate of two hundred and fifty pounds a job. Plus bonuses in cases where the divorce settlement proved suitably substantial. A bit like a lawyer's contingency fee. No win, no fee.'

I can't quite get my head round this idea. 'So it would work how? You'd bell me and tell me where to do the business?'

Sarah shakes her head. 'It would all go through Chrissie. She'll give you the details, then she'll bill the legal firms for miscellaneous services, and pass the fees on to you. After this meeting, we'll never talk about this again face to face. And you'll never have contact with the solicitors you'd be acting for. Chrissie's the cut-out on both sides.'

'What do you think, Tel?' Chrissie asks, eager as a virgin in the back seat.

'You could tell Kimmy you were doing process serving,' Sarah chips in.

That's the clincher. So I say OK.

That was six months ago. Now I'm on Chrissie's books as her research assistant. I pay tax and National Insurance, which was a bit of a facer for the social security, who could not get their heads round the idea of me as a proper citizen. I do two or three jobs a week, and everything's sweet.

Sarah's sorting out Kimmy's divorce, and we're getting married as soon as all that's sorted.

I tell you, this is the life. I'm doing the right thing and I get paid for it. If I'd known going straight could be this much fun, I'd have done it years ago.

A Wife in a Million

The woman strolled through the supermarket, choosing a few items for her basket. As she reached the display of sauces and pickles, a muscle in her jaw tightened. She looked around, willing herself to appear casual. No one watched. Swiftly she took a jar of tomato pickle from her large leather handbag and placed it on the shelf. She moved on to the frozen meat section.

A few minutes later, she passed down the same aisle and paused. She repeated the exercise, this time adding two more jars to the shelf. As she walked on to the checkout, she felt tension slide from her body, leaving her light-headed.

She stood in the queue, anonymous among the morning shoppers, another neat woman in a well-cut winter coat, a faint smile on her face and a strangely unfocused look in her pale blue eyes.

Sarah Graham was sprawled on the sofa reading the Situations Vacant in the *Burnalder Evening News* when she heard the car pull up the drive. Sighing, she dropped the paper and went through to the kitchen. By the time she had pulled the cork from a bottle of elderflower wine and poured two glasses, the front door had opened and closed. Sarah stood, glasses in hand, facing the kitchen door.

Detective Sergeant Maggie Staniforth came into the kitchen, took the proffered glass and kissed Sarah perfunctorily. She walked into the living-room and slumped in a chair, calling over her shoulder, 'And what kind of day have you had?'

Sarah followed her through and shrugged. 'Another shitty day in paradise. You don't want to hear my catalogue of boredom.'

'You never bore me. And besides, it does me good to be reminded that there's a life outside crime.'

'I got up about nine, by which time you'd probably arrested half a dozen villains. I whizzed through the *Guardian* job ads, and went down the library to check out the other papers. After lunch I cleaned the bedroom, did a bit of ironing and polished the dining-room furniture. Then down to the newsagent's for the evening paper. A thrill a minute. And you? Solved the crime of the century?'

Maggie winced. 'Nothing so exciting. Bit of breaking and entering, bit of paperwork on the rape case at the blues club. It's due in court next week.'

'At least you get paid for it.'

'Something will come up soon, love.'

'And meanwhile I go on being your kept woman.'

Maggie said nothing. There was nothing to say. The two of them had been together since they fell head over heels in love at university eleven years before. Things had been fine while they were both concentrating on climbing their career ladders. But Sarah's career in personnel management had hit a brick wall when the company that employed her had collapsed nine months previously. That crisis had opened a wound in their relationship that was rapidly festering. Now Maggie was often afraid to speak for fear of provoking another bitter exchange. She drank her wine in silence.

'No titbits to amuse me, then?' Sarah demanded. 'No funny little tales from the underbelly?'

'One that might interest you,' Maggie said tentatively. 'Notice a story in the *News* last night about a woman taken to the General with suspected food poisoning?'

'I saw it. I read every inch of that paper. It fills an hour.'

'Well, she's died. The news came in just as I was leaving. And there have apparently been another two families affected. The funny thing is that there doesn't seem to be a common source. Jim Bryant from casualty was telling me about it.'

Sarah pulled a face. 'Sure you can face my spaghetti carbonara tonight?'

The telephone cut across Maggie's smile. She quickly crossed the room and picked it up on the third ring. 'DS Staniforth speaking . . . Hi, Bill.' She listened intently. 'Good God!' she exclaimed. 'I'll be with you in ten minutes. OK?' She stood holding the phone. 'Sarah . . . that woman we were just talking about. It wasn't food poisoning. It was a massive dose of arsenic and two of the other so-called food poisoning cases have died. They suspect arsenic there too. I've got to go and meet Bill at the hospital.'

'You'd better get a move on, then. Shall I save you some food?'

'No point. And don't wait up, I'll be late.' Maggie crossed to Sarah and gave her a brief hug. She hurried out of the room. Seconds later, the front door slammed.

The fluorescent strips made the kitchen look bright but cold. The woman opened one of the fitted cupboards and took a jar of greyish-white powder from the very back of the shelf.

She picked up a filleting knife whose edge was honed to a

wicked sharpness. She slid it delicately under the flap of a cardboard pack of blancmange powder. She did the same to five other packets. Then she carefully opened the inner paper envelopes. Into each she mixed a tablespoonful of the powder from the jar.

Under the light, the grey strands in her auburn hair glinted. Painstakingly, she folded the inner packets closed again and with a drop of glue she resealed the cardboard packages. She put them all in a shopping bag and carried it into the rear porch.

She replaced the jar in the cupboard and went through to the living-room where the television blared. She looked strangely triumphant.

It was after three when Maggie Staniforth closed the front door behind her. As she hung up her sheepskin, she noticed lines of strain round her eyes in the hall mirror. Sarah appeared in the kitchen doorway. 'I know you're probably too tired to feel hungry, but I've made some soup if you want it,' she said.

'You shouldn't have stayed up. It's late.'

'I've got nothing else to do. After all, there's plenty of opportunity for me to catch up on my sleep.'

Please God, not now, thought Maggie. As if the job isn't hard enough without coming home to hassles from Sarah.

But she was proved wrong. Sarah smiled and said, 'So do you want some grub?'

'That depends.'

'On what?'

'Whether there's Higham's Continental Tomato Pickle in it.'

Sarah looked bewildered. Maggie went on. 'It seems that three people have died from arsenic administered in Higham's Continental Tomato Pickle bought from Fastfare Supermarket.'

'You're joking!'

'Wish I was.' Maggie went through to the kitchen. She poured herself a glass of orange juice as Sarah served up a steaming bowl of lentil soup with a pile of buttered brown bread. Maggie sat down and tucked in, giving her lover a disjointed summary as she ate.

'Victim number one: May Scott, fifty-seven, widow, lived up Warburton Road. Numbers two and three: Gary Andrews, fifteen, and his brother Kevin, thirteen, from Priory Farm Estate. Their father is seriously ill. So are two others now, Thomas and Louise Foster of Bryony Grange. No connection between them except that they all ate pickle from jars bought on the same day at Fastfare.

'Could be someone playing at extortion – you know, pay me a million pounds or I'll do it again. Could be someone with a grudge against Fastfare. Ditto against Higham's. So you can bet your sweet life we're going to be hammered into the ground on this one. Already we're getting flak.'

Maggie finished her meal. Her head dropped into her hands. 'What a bitch of a job.'

'Better than no job at all.'

'Is it?'

'You should know better than to ask.'

Maggie sighed. 'Take me to bed, Sarah. Let me forget about the battlefield for a few hours, eh?'

* * *

Piped music lulled the shoppers at Pinkerton's Hypermarket into a drugged acquisitiveness. The woman pushing the trolley was deaf to its bland presence and its blandishments. When she reached the shelf with the instant desserts on display, she stopped and checked that the coast was clear.

She swiftly put three packs of blancmange on the shelf with their fellows and moved away. A few minutes later she returned and studied several cake mixes as she waited for the aisle to clear. Then she completed her mission and finished her shopping in a leisurely fashion.

At the checkout she chatted brightly to the bored teenager who rang up her purchases automatically. Then she left, gently humming the song that flowed from the shop's speakers.

Three days later, Maggie Staniforth burst into her living-room in the middle of the afternoon to find Sarah typing a job application. 'Red alert, love,' she announced. 'I'm only home to have a quick bath and change my things. Any chance of a sandwich?'

'I was beginning to wonder if you still lived here,' Sarah muttered darkly. 'If you were having an affair, at least I'd know how to fight back.'

'Not now, love, please.'

'Do you want something hot? Soup? Omelette?'

'Soup, please. And a toasted cheese sandwich?'

'Coming up. What's the panic this time?'

Maggie's eyes clouded. 'Our homicidal maniac has struck again. Eight people on the critical list at the General. This time the arsenic was in Garratt's Blancmange from Pinkerton's Hypermarket. Bill's doing a television appeal right now asking for people to bring in any packets bought there this week.'

'Different manufacturer, different supermarket. Sounds like a crazy rather than a grudge, doesn't it?'

'And that makes the next strike impossible to predict. Anyway, I'm going for that bath now. I'll be down again in fifteen minutes.' Maggie stopped in the kitchen doorway, 'I'm not being funny, Sarah. Don't do any shopping in the supermarkets. Butchers, greengrocers, okay. But no self-service, pre-packaged food. Please.'

Sarah nodded. She had never seen Maggie afraid in eight years in the force, and the sight did nothing to life her depressed spirits.

This time it was jars of mincemeat. Even the Salvation Army band playing carols outside the Nationwide Stores failed to make the woman pause in her mission. Her shopping bag held six jars laced with deadly white powder when she entered the supermarket.

When she left, there were none. She dropped 50p in the collecting tin as she passed the band because they were playing her favourite carol, 'In the Bleak Midwinter'. She walked slowly back to the car park, not pausing to look at the shop-window Christmas displays. She wasn't anticipating a merry Christmas.

Sarah walked back from the newsagent's with the evening paper, reading the front page as she went. The Burnalder Poisoner was front-page news everywhere by now, but the stories in the local paper seemed to carry an extra edge of fear. They were thorough in their coverage, tracing any possible commercial connection between the three giant food companies that produced the contaminated food. They also speculated on the possible reasons for the week-long gaps between outbreaks. They laid out in stark detail the drastic effect the poisoning was having on the finances of the food-processing companies. And they noted the paradox of public hysteria about the poisoning while people still filled their shopping trolleys in anticipation of the festive season.

The latest killer was Univex mincemeat. Sarah shivered as she read of the latest three deaths, bringing the toll to twelve. As she turned the corner, she saw Maggie's car in the drive and increased her pace. A grim idea had taken root in her brain as she read the long report.

While she was hanging up her jacket, Maggie called from the kitchen. Sarah walked slowly through to find her tucking into a plate of eggs and bacon, but without her usual large dollop of tomato ketchup. There were dark circles beneath her eyes and the skin around them was grey and stretched. She had not slept at home for two nights. The job had never made such demands on her before. Sarah found a moment to wonder if the atmosphere between them was partly responsible for Maggie's total commitment to this desperate search.

'How is it going?' she asked anxiously.

'It's not,' said Maggie. 'Virtually nothing to go on. No link that we can find. It's not as if we even have proper leads to chase up. I came home for a break because we were just sitting staring at each other, wondering what to do next. Short of searching everyone who goes into the supermarkets, what can we do? And those bloody reporters seem to have taken up residence in the station. We're being leaned on from all sides. We've got to crack this soon or we'll be crucified.'

Sarah sat down. 'I've been giving this some thought. The grudge theory has broken down because you can't find a link between the companies, am I right?'

'Yes.'

'Have you thought about the effect unemployment has on crime?'

'Burglary, shoplifting, mugging, vandalism, drugs, yes. But surely not mass poisoning, love.'

'There's so much bitterness there, Maggie. So much hatred. I've often felt like murdering those incompetent tossers who destroyed Liddell's and threw me on the scrapheap. Did you think about people who've been given the boot?'

'We did think about it. But only a handful of people have worked for all three companies. None of them have any reason to hold a grudge. And none of them have any connection with Burnalder.'

'There's another aspect, though, Maggie. It only hit me when I read the paper tonight. The *News* has a big piece about the parent companies who make the three products. Now, I'd swear that each one of those companies has advertised in the last couple of months for management executives. I know, I applied for two of the jobs. I didn't even get interviewed because I've got no experience in the food industry, only in plastics. There must be other people in the same boat, maybe less stable than I am.'

'My God!' Maggie breathed. She pushed her plate away. The colour had returned to her cheeks and she seemed to have found fresh energy. She got up and hugged Sarah fiercely. 'You've given us the first positive lead in this whole bloody case. You're a genius!'

'I hope you'll remember that when they give you your inspector's job.'

Maggie grinned on her way out the door. 'I owe you one. I'll see you later.'

As the front door slammed, Sarah said ironically, 'I hope it's not too late already, babe.'

Detective Inspector Bill Nicholson had worked with Maggie Staniforth for two years. His initial distrust of her gender had been broken down by her sheer grasp of the job. Now he was wont to describe her as 'a bloody good copper in spite of being a woman', as if this were a discovery uniquely his, and a direct product of working for him. As she unfolded Sarah's suggestion, backed by photostats of newspaper advertisements culled from the local paper's files, he realised for the first time she was probably going to leapfrog him on the career ladder before too long. He didn't like the idea, but he wasn't prepared to let that stand between him and a job of work.

They started on the long haul of speaking directly to the personnel officers of the three companies. It meant quartering the country and they knew they were working against the clock. Back in Burnalder, a team of detectives was phoning companies who had advertised similar vacancies, asking for lists of applicants. The lumbering machinery of the law was in gear.

On the evening of the second day, an exhausted Maggie arrived home. Six hundred and thirty-seven miles of driving had taken their toll and she looked crumpled and older by ten years. Sarah helped her out of her coat and poured her a stiff drink in silence.

'You were right,' Maggie sighed. 'We've got the name and address of a man who has been rejected by all three firms after the first interview. We're moving in on him tonight. If he sticks to his pattern, he'll be aiming to strike again tomorrow. So with luck, it'll be a red-handed job.' She sounded grim and distant. 'What a bloody waste. Twelve lives because he can't get a bloody job.'

'I can understand it,' Sarah said abruptly and went through to the kitchen.

Maggie stared after her, shocked but comprehending. She felt again the low rumble of anger inside her against a system that set her to catch the people it had so often made its victims. If only Sarah had not lost her well-paid job, then Maggie knew she would have left the force by now, but they needed her salary to keep their heads above water. The job itself was dirty enough; but the added pain of keeping her relationship with Sarah constantly under wraps was gradually becoming more than she could comfortably bear. Sarah wasn't the only one whose choices had been drastically pruned by her unemployment.

By nine fifty-five a dozen detectives were stationed around a neat detached house in a quiet suburban street. In the garden a 'For Sale' sign sprouted among the rose bushes. Lights burned in the kitchen and living-room.

In the car, Bill made a final check of the search warrant. Then, after a last word over the radio, he and Maggie walked up the short drive.

'It's up to you now,' he said and rang the doorbell. It was answered by a tall, bluff man in his mid-forties. There were lines of strain round his eyes and his clothes hung loosely, as if he had recently lost weight.

'Yes?' he asked in a pleasant, gentle voice.

'Mr Derek Millfield?' Maggie demanded.

'That's me. How can I help you?'

'We're police officers, Mr Millfield. We'd like to have a word with you, if you don't mind.'

He looked puzzled. 'By all means. But I don't see what . . .' His voice tailed off. 'You'd better come in, I suppose.'

They entered the house and Millfield showed them into a surprisingly large living-room. It was tastefully and expensively furnished. A woman sat watching television.

'My wife Shula,' he explained. 'Shula, these are policemen – I mean officers. Sorry, miss.'

Shula Millfield stood up and faced them. 'You've come for me, then,' she said.

It was hard to say who looked most surprised. Then suddenly she was laughing, crying and screaming, all at once.

Maggie stretched out on the sofa. 'It was appalling. She must have been living on a knife-edge for weeks before she finally flipped. He's been out of work for seven months. They've had to take their kids out of private school, had to sell a car, sell their possessions. He had no idea what she was up to. I've never seen anyone go berserk like that. All for the sake of a nice middle-class lifestyle.

'There's no doubt about her guilt, either. Her fingerprints are all over the jar of arsenic. She stole the jar a month ago. She worked part-time in the pharmacy at the cottage hospital in Kingcaple. But they didn't notice the loss. God knows how. Deputy-heads will roll,' she added bitterly.

'What will happen to her?' Sarah asked coolly.

'She'll be tried, if she's fit to plead. But I doubt if she will be. I'm afraid it'll be the locked ward for life.' When she looked up, Maggie saw there were tears on Sarah's cheeks. She immediately got up and put an arm round her. 'Hey, don't cry, love. Please.'

'I can't help it, Maggie. You see, I know how she feels. I know that utter lack of all hope. I know that hatred, that sense of frustration and futility. There's nothing you can do to take that away. What you have to live with, Detective-Sergeant Staniforth, is that it could have been me.

'It could so easily have been me.'

A Traditional Christmas

 Last night, I dreamed I went to Amberley. Snow had fallen, deep and crisp and even, garlanding the trees like tinsel sparkling in the sunlight as we swept through the tall iron gates and up the drive. Diana was driving, her gloved hands assured on the wheel in spite of the hazards of an imperfectly cleared surface. We rounded the coppice, and there was the house, perfect as a photograph, the sun seeming to breathe life into the golden Cotswold stone. Amberley House, one of the little jobs Vanbrugh knocked off once he'd learned the trade with Blenheim Palace.

Diana stopped in front of the portico and blared the horn. She turned to me, eyes twinkling, smile bewitching as ever. 'Christmas begins here,' she said. As if on cue, the front door opened and Edmund stood framed in the doorway, flanked by his and Diana's mother, and his wife Jane, all smiling as gaily as daytrippers.

I woke then, rigid with shock, pop-eyed in the dark. It was one of those dreams so vivid that when you waken, you can't quite believe it has just happened. But I knew it was a dream. A nightmare, rather. For Edmund, sixth Baron Amberley of Anglezarke had been dead for three months. I should know. I found the body.

Beside me, Diana was still asleep. I wanted to burrow into her side, seeking comfort from the horrors of memory, but I couldn't bring myself to be so selfish. A proper night's sleep was still a luxury for her and the next couple of weeks weren't exactly going to be restful. I slipped out of bed and went through to the kitchen to make a cup of camomile tea.

I huddled over the gas fire and forced myself to think back to Christmas. It was the fourth year that Diana and I had made the trip back to her ancestral home to celebrate. As our first Christmas together had approached, I'd worried about what we were going to do. In relationships like ours, there isn't a standard formula. The only thing I was sure about was that I wanted us to spend it together. I knew that meant visiting my parents was out. As long as they never have to confront the physical evidence of my lesbianism, they can handle it. Bringing any woman home to their tenement flat in Glasgow for Christmas would be uncomfortable. Bringing the daughter of a baron would be impossible.

When I'd nervously broached the subject, Diana had looked astonished, her eyebrows raised, her mouth twitching in a half-smile. 'I assumed you'd want to come to Amberley with me,' she said. 'They're expecting you to.'

'Are you sure?'

Diana grabbed me in a bear-hug. 'Of course I'm sure. Don't you want to spend Christmas with me?'

'Stupid question,' I grunted. 'I thought maybe we could celebrate on our own, just the two of us. Romantic, intimate, that sort of thing.'

Diana looked uncertain. 'Can't we be romantic at Amberley? I can't imagine Christmas anywhere else. It's so . . . traditional. So English.'

My turn for the raised eyebrows. 'Sure I'll fit in?'

'You know my mother thinks the world of you. She insists

on you coming. She's fanatical about tradition, especially Christmas. You'll love it,' she promised.

And I did. Unlikely as it is, this Scottish working-class lesbian feminist homeopath fell head over heels for the whole English country-house package. I loved driving down with Diana on Christmas Eve, leaving the motorway traffic behind, slipping through narrow lanes with their tall hedgerows, driving through the chocolate-box village of Amberley, fairy lights strung round the green, and, finally, cruising past the Dower House where her mother lived and on up the drive. I loved the sherry and mince pies with the neighbours, even the ones who wanted to regale me with their ailments. I loved the elaborate Christmas Eve meal Diana's mother cooked. I loved the brisk walk through the woods to the village church for the midnight service. I loved most of all the way they simply absorbed me into their ritual without distance.

Christmas Day was champagne breakfast, stockings crammed with childish toys and expensive goodies from the Sloane Ranger shops, church again, then presents proper. The gargantuan feast of Christmas dinner, with free-range turkey from the estate's home farm. Then a dozen close family friends arrived to pull crackers, wear silly hats and masks, drink like tomorrow was another life and play every ridiculous party game from Sardines to Charades. I'm glad no one's ever videotaped the evening and threatened to send a copy to the women's alternative health co-operative where I practise. I'd have to pay the blackmail. Diana and I lead a classless life in London, where almost no one knows her background. It's not that she's embarrassed. It's just that she knows from bitter experience how many barriers it builds for her. But at Amberley, we left behind my homeopathy and her Legal Aid practice, and for a few days we lived in a time warp that Charles Dickens would have revelled in.

On Boxing Day night, we always trooped down to the village hall for the dance. It was then that Edmund came into his own. His huntin', shootin' and fishin' persona slipped from him like the masks we'd worn the night before when he picked up his alto sax and stepped onto the stage to lead the twelve-piece Amber Band. Most of his fellow members were professional session musicians, but the drummer doubled as a labourer on Amberley Farm and the keyboard player was the village postman. I'm no connoisseur, but I reckoned the Amber Band was one of the best live outfits I've ever heard. They played everything from Duke Ellington to Glenn Miller, including Miles Davis and John Coltrane pieces, all arranged by Edmund. And of course, they played some of Edmund's own compositions, strange haunting slow-dancing pieces that somehow achieved the seemingly impossible marriage between the English countryside and jazz.

There was nothing different to mark out last Christmas as a watershed gig. Edmund led the band with his usual verve. Diana and I danced with each other half the night and took it in turns to dance with her mother the rest of the time. Evangeline ('call me Evie') still danced with a vivacity and flair that made me understand why Diana's father had fallen for her. As usual, Jane sat stolidly nursing a gin and tonic that she made last the whole night. 'I don't dance,' she'd said stiffly to me when I'd asked her up on my first visit. It was a rebuff that brooked no argument. Later, I asked Diana if Jane had knocked me back because I was a dyke.

Diana roared with laughter. 'Good God, no,' she spluttered. 'Jane doesn't even dance with Edmund. She's tone deaf and has no sense of rhythm.'

'Bit of a handicap, being married to Edmund,' I said.

Diana shrugged. 'It would be if music were the only thing he did. But the Amber Band only does a few gigs a year. The rest of the time he's running the estate and Jane loves being the country squire's wife.'

In the intervening years, that was the only thing that had changed. Word of mouth had increased the demand for the Amber Band's services. By last Christmas, the band were playing at least one gig a week. They'd moved up from playing village halls and hunt balls onto the student-union circuit.

Last Christmas I'd gone for a walk with Diana's mother on the afternoon of Christmas Eve. As we'd emerged from the back door, I noticed a three-ton van parked over by the stables. Along the side, in tall letters of gold and black, it said, 'Amber Band! Bringing jazz to the people.'

'Wow,' I said, 'That looks serious.'

Evie laughed. 'It keeps Edmund happy. His father was obsessed with breaking the British record for the largest salmon, which, believe me, was a far more inconvenient interest than Edmund's. All Jane has to put up with is a lack of Edmund's company two or three nights a week at most. Going alone to a dinner party is a far lighter cross to bear than being dragged off to fishing lodges in the middle of nowhere to be bitten to death by midges.'

'Doesn't he find it hard, trying to run the estate as well?' I asked idly as we struck out across the park towards the coppice.

Evie's lips pursed momentarily, but her voice betrayed no irritation. 'He's taken a man on part-time to take care of the day-to-day business. Edmund keeps his hands firmly on the reins, but Lewis has taken on the burden of much of the routine work.'

'It can't be easy, making an estate like this pay nowadays.'

Evie smiled. 'Edmund's very good at it. He understands the importance of tradition, but he's not afraid to try new things. I'm very lucky with my children, Jo. They've turned out better than any mother could have hoped.'

I accepted the implied compliment in silence.

The happy family idyll crashed around everyone's ears the day after Boxing Day. Edmund had seemed quieter than usual over lunch, but I put that down to the hangover that, if there were any justice in the world, he should be suffering. As Evie poured out the coffee, he cleared his throat and said abruptly, 'I've got something to say to you all.'

Diana and I exchanged questioning looks. I noticed Jane's face freeze, her fingers clutching the handle of her coffee cup. Evie finished what she was doing and sat down. 'We're all listening, Edmund,' she said gently.

'As you're all aware, Amber Band has become increasingly successful. A few weeks ago, I was approached by a representative of a major record company. They would like us to sign a deal with them to make some recordings. They would also like to help us move our touring venues up a gear or two. I've discussed this with the band, and we're all agreed that we would be crazy to turn our backs on this opportunity.' Edmund paused and looked around apprehensively.

'Congratulations, bro,' Diana said. I could hear the nervousness in her voice, though I wasn't sure why she was so apprehensive. I sat silent, waiting for the other shoe to drop.

'Go on,' Evie said in a voice so unemotional it sent a chill to my heart.

'Obviously, this is something that has implications for Amberley. I can't have a career as a musician and continue to be responsible for all of this. Also, we need to increase the income from the estate in order to make sure that whatever happens to my career, there will always be enough money available to allow Ma to carry on as she has always done. So I have made the decision to hand over the running of the house and the estate to a management company who will run the house as a residential conference centre and manage the land in broad accordance with the principles I've already established,' Edmund said in a rush.

Jane's face flushed dark red. 'How dare you?' she hissed. 'You can't turn this place into some bloody talking shop. The house will be full of ghastly sales reps. Our lives won't be our own.'

Edmund looked down at the table. 'We won't be here,' he said softly. 'It makes more sense if we move out. I thought we could take a house in London.' He looked up beseechingly at Jane, a look so naked it was embarrassing to witness it.

'This is extraordinary,' Evie said, finding her voice at last. 'Hundreds of years of tradition, and you want to smash it to pieces to indulge some hobby?'

Edmund took a deep breath. 'Ma, it's not a hobby. It's the only time I feel properly alive. Look, this is not a matter for discussion. I've made my mind up. The house and the estate are mine absolutely to do with as I see fit, and these are my plans. There's no point in argument. The papers are all drawn up and I'm going to town tomorrow to sign them. The other chaps from the village have already handed in their notice. We're all set.'

Jane stood up. 'You bastard,' she yelled. 'You inconsiderate bastard! Why didn't you discuss this with me?'

Edmund raised his hands out to her. 'I knew you'd be opposed to it. And you know how hard I find it to say no to you. Jane, I need to do this. It'll be fine, I promise you. We'll find somewhere lovely to live in London, near your friends.'

Wordlessly, Jane picked up her coffee cup and hurled it at Edmund. It caught him in the middle of the forehead. He barely flinched as the hot liquid poured down his face, turning his sweater brown. 'You insensitive pig,' she said in a low voice. 'Hadn't you noticed I haven't had a period for two months? I'm pregnant, Edmund, you utter bastard. I'm two months pregnant and you want to turn my life upside down?' Then she ran from the room slamming the heavy door behind her, no mean feat in itself.

In the stunned silence that followed Jane's bombshell, no one moved. Then Edmund, his face seeming to disintegrate, pushed his chair back with a screech and hurried wordlessly after his wife. I turned to look at Diana. The sight of her stricken face was like a blow to the chest. I barely registered Evie sighing, 'How sharper than a serpent's tooth,' before she too left the room. Before the door closed behind her, I was out of my chair, Diana pressed close to me.

Dinner that evening was the first meal I'd eaten at Amberley in an atmosphere of strain. Hardly a word was spoken, and I suspect I wasn't alone in feeling relief when Edmund rose abruptly before coffee and announced he was going down to the village to rehearse. 'Don't wait up,' he said tersely.

Jane went upstairs as soon as the meal was over. Evie sat down with us to watch a film, but half an hour into it, she rose and said, 'I'm sorry. I'm not concentrating. Your brother has given me rather too much to think about. I'm going back to the Dower House.'

Diana and I walked to the door with her mother. We stood under the portico, watching the dark figure against the snow. The air was heavy, the sky lowering. 'Feels like a storm brewing,' Diana remarked. 'Even the weather's cross with Edmund.'

We watched the rest of the film then decided to go up to bed. As we walked through the hall, I went to switch off the lights on the Christmas tree. 'Leave them,' Diana said. 'Edmund will turn them off when he comes in. It's tradition – last to bed does the tree.' She smiled reminiscently. 'The number of times I've come back from parties in the early hours and seen the tree shining down the drive.'

About an hour later, the storm broke. We were reading in bed when a clap of thunder as loud as a bomb blast crashed over the house. Then a rattle of machine-gun fire against the window. We clutched each other in surprise, though heaven knows we've never needed an excuse. Diana slipped out of bed and pulled back one of the heavy damask curtains so we could watch the hail pelt the window and the bolts of lightning flash jagged across the sky. It raged for nearly half an hour. Diana and I played the game of counting the gap between thunderclaps and lightning flashes, which told us the storm seemed to be circling Amberley itself, moving off only to come back and blast us again with lightning and hail.

Eventually it moved off to the west, occasional flashes lighting up the distant hills. Somehow, it seemed the right time to make love. As we lay together afterwards, revelling in the luxury of satiated sensuality, the lights suddenly went out. 'Damn,' Diana drawled. 'Bloody storm's got the electrics on the blink.' She stirred. 'I'd better go down and check the fuse box.'

I grabbed her. 'Leave it,' I urged. 'Edmund can do it when he comes in. We're all warm and sleepy. Besides, I might get lonely.'

Diana chuckled and snuggled back into my arms. Moments later, the lights came back on again. 'See?' I said. 'No need. Probably a problem at the local sub-station because of the weather.'

I woke up just after seven the following morning, full of the joys of spring. We were due to go back to London after lunch, so I decided to sneak out for an early morning walk in the copse. I dressed without waking Diana and slipped out of the silent house.

The path from the house to the copse was well-trodden. There had been no fresh snow since Christmas Eve, and the path was well used, since it was a short cut both to the Dower House and the village. There were even mountain-bike tracks among the scattered boot prints. The trees, an elderly mixture of beech, birch, alder, oak and ash, still held their tracery of snow on the tops of some branches, though following the storm a mild thaw had set in. As I moved into the wood, I felt drips of melting snow on my head.

In the middle of the copse, there's a clearing fringed with silver birch trees. When she was little, Diana was convinced this was the place where the fairies came to recharge their magic. There was no magic in the clearing that morning. As soon as I emerged from the trees, I saw Edmund's body, sprawled under a single silver birch tree by the path on the far side.

For a moment, I was frozen with shock. Then I rushed forward and crouched down beside him. I didn't need to feel for a pulse. He was clearly long dead, his right hand blackened and burned.

I can't remember the next hours. Apparently, I went to the Dower House and roused Evie. I blurted out what I'd seen and she called the police. I have a vague recollection of her staggering slightly as I broke the news, but I was in shock and I have no recollection of what she said. Diana arrived soon afterwards. When her mother told her what had happened, she stared numbly at me for a moment, then tears poured down her face. None of us seemed eager to be the one to break the news to Jane. Eventually, as if by mutual consent, we waited until the police arrived. We merited two uniformed constables, plus two plain-clothes detectives. In the words of Noël Coward, Detective Inspector Maggie Staniforth would not have fooled a drunken child of two and a half. As soon as Evie introduced me as her daughter's partner, DI Staniforth thawed visibly. I didn't much care at that point. I was too numbed even to take in what they were saying. It sounded like the distant mutter of bees in a herb garden.

DI Staniforth set off with her team to examine the body

while Diana and I, after a muttered discussion in the corner, informed Evie that we would go and tell Jane. We found her in the kitchen drinking a mug of coffee. 'I don't suppose you've seen my husband,' she said in tones of utter contempt when we walked in. 'He didn't have the courage to come home last night.'

Diana sat down next to Jane and flashed me a look of panic. I stepped forward. 'I'm sorry, Jane, but there's been an accident.' In moments of crisis, why is it we always reach for the nearest cliché?

Jane looked at me as if I were speaking Swahili. 'An accident?' she asked in a macabre echo of Dame Edith Evans's 'A handbag?'

'Edmund's dead,' Diana blurted out. 'He was struck by lightning in the wood. Coming home from the village.'

As she spoke, a wave of nausea surged through me. I thought I was going to faint. I grabbed the edge of the table. Diana's words robbed the muscles in my legs of their strength and I lurched into the nearest chair. Up until that point, I'd been too dazed with shock to realise the conclusion everyone but me had come to.

Jane looked blankly at Diana. 'I'm so sorry,' Diana said, the tears starting again, flowing down her cheeks.

'I'm not,' Jane said. 'He can't stop my child growing up in Amberley now.'

Diana turned white. 'You bitch,' she said wonderingly.

At least I knew then what I had to do.

Maggie Staniforth arrived shortly after to interview me. 'It's just a formality,' she said. 'It's obvious what happened. He was walking home in the storm and was struck by lightning as he passed under the birch tree.'

I took a deep breath. 'I'm afraid not,' I said. 'Edmund was murdered.'

Her eyebrows rose. 'You're still in shock. I'm afraid there are no suspicious circumstances.'

'Maybe not to you. But I know different.'

Credit where it's due, she heard me out. But the sceptical look never left her eyes. 'That's all very well,' she said eventually. 'But if what you're saying is true, there's no way of proving it.'

I shrugged. 'Why don't you look for fingerprints? Either in the plug of the Christmas tree lights, or on the main fuse box. When he was electrocuted, the lights fused. At the time, Diana and I thought it was a glitch in the mains supply, but we know better now. Jane would have had to rewire the plug and the socket to cover her tracks. And she must have gone down to the cellar to repair the fuse or turn the circuit breaker back on. She wouldn't have had occasion to touch those in the usual run of things. I doubt she'd even have good reason to know where the fuse box is. Try it,' I urged.

And that's how Evie came to be charged with the murder of her son. If I'd thought things through, if I'd waited till my brain was out of shock, I'd have realised that Jane would never have risked her baby by hauling Edmund's body over the crossbar of his mountain bike and wheeling him out to the copse. Besides, she probably believed she could use his love for her to persuade him to change his mind. Evie didn't have that hope to cling to.

If I'd realised it was Diana's mother who killed Edmund, I doubt very much if I'd have shared my esoteric knowledge with DI Staniforth. It's a funny business, New Age medicine. When I attended a seminar on the healing powers of plants given by a Native American medicine man, I never thought his wisdom would help me prove a murder.

Maybe Evie will get lucky. Maybe she'll get a jury reluctant to convict in a case that rests on the inexplicable fact that lightning never strikes birch trees.

The Girl Who Killed Santa Claus

It was the night before Christmas, and not surprisingly, Kelly Jane Davidson was wide awake. It wasn't that she wanted to be. It wasn't as if she believed in Santa and expected to catch him coming down the chimney onto the coal-effect gas fire in the living-room. After all, she was nearly eight now.

She felt scornful as she thought back to last Christmas when she'd still been a baby, a mere six year old who still believed that there really was an elf factory in Lapland where they made the toys; that there really was a team of reindeer who magically pulled a sleigh across the skies and somehow got round all the world's children with sackloads of gifts; that she could really write a letter to Santa and he'd personally choose and deliver her presents.

Of course, she'd known for ages before then that the fat men in red suits and false beards who sat her on their knees in an assortment of gaudy grottoes weren't the real Santa. They were just men who dressed up and acted as messengers for the real Father Christmas, passing on her desires and giving her a token of what would be waiting for her on Christmas morning.

She'd had her suspicions about the rest of the story, so when Simon Sharp had told her in the playground that there wasn't really a Santa Claus, she hadn't even felt shocked or shaken. She hadn't tried to argue, not like her best friend

Sarah, who had gone red in the face and looked like she was going to burst into tears. But it was obvious when you thought about it. Her mum was always complaining when she ordered things from catalogues and they sent the wrong thing. If the catalogue people couldn't get a simple order right, how could one fat man and a bunch of elves get the right toys to all the children in the world on one night?

So Kelly Jane had said goodbye to Santa without a moment's regret. She might have been more worried if she hadn't discovered the secret of the airing cupboard. Her mum had been downstairs making the tea, and Kelly Jane had wanted a pillowcase to make a sleeping bag for her favourite doll. She'd opened the airing cupboard and there, on the top shelf, she'd seen a stack of strangely shaped plastic bags. They were too high for her to reach, but she'd craned her neck and managed to see the corner of some packaging inside one of the bags. Her heart had started to pound with excitement, for she'd immediately recognised the familiar box that she'd been staring at in longing in the toyshop window for weeks.

She'd closed the door silently and crept back to her room. Her mum had said, 'Wait and see what Santa brings you,' as if she was still a silly baby when she'd asked for the new Barbie doll. But here it was in the house.

Later, when her mum and dad were safely shut in the living-room watching the telly, she'd crept out of bed and used the chair from her bedroom to climb up and explore further. It had left her feeling very satisfied. Santa or no Santa, she was going to have a great Christmas.

Which was why she couldn't sleep. The prospect of playing with her new toys, not to mention showing them off to

Sarah, was too exciting to let her drift off into dreams. Restless, she got out of bed and pulled the curtains open. It was a cold, clear night, and in spite of the city lights, she could still see the stars twinkling, the thin crescent of the moon like a knife cut in the dark blue of the sky. No sleigh, or reindeers, though.

She had no idea how much time had passed when she heard the footsteps. Heavy, uneven thuds on the stairs. Not the light-footed tread of her mum, nor the measured foot-falls of her dad. These were stumbling steps, irregular and clumsy, as if someone was negotiating unfamiliar territory.

Kelly Jane was suddenly aware how cold it had become. Her arms and legs turned to gooseflesh, the short hair on the back of her neck prickling with unease. Who – or what – was out there, in her house, in the middle of the night?

She heard a bump and a muffled voice grunting, as if in pain. It didn't sound like anyone she knew. It didn't even sound human. More like an animal. Or some sort of monster, like in the stories they'd read at school at Hallowe'en. Trolls that ate little children. She'd remembered the trolls, and for weeks she'd taken the long way home to avoid going over the ring-road flyover. She knew it wasn't a proper bridge like trolls lived under, but she didn't want to take any chances. Sarah had agreed with her, though Simon Sharp had laughed at the pair of them. It would have served him right to have a troll in his house on Christmas Eve. It wasn't fair that it had come to her house, Kelly Jane thought, trying to make herself angry to drive the fear away.

It didn't work. Her stomach hurt. She'd never been this scared, not even when she had to have a filling at the dentist. She wanted to hide in her wardrobe, but she knew it was silly to go somewhere she could be trapped so easily. Besides, she had to know the worst.

On tiptoe, she crossed the room, blinking back tears. Cautiously, she turned the door handle and inched the door open. The landing light was off, but she could just make out a bulky shape standing by the airing cupboard. As her eyes adjusted to the deeper darkness, she could see an arm stretching up to the top shelf. It clutched the packages and put them in a sack. Her packages! Her Christmas presents!

With terrible clarity, Kelly Jane realised that this was no monster. It was a burglar, pure and simple. A bad man had broken into her house and was stealing her Christmas presents! Outrage flooded through her, banishing fear in that instant. As the bulky figure put the last parcel in his sack and turned back to the stairs, she launched herself through the door and raced down the landing, crashing into the burglar's legs just as he took the first step. 'Go away, you bad burglar,' she screamed.

Caught off balance, he crashed head over heels down the stairs, a yell of surprise splitting the silence of the night like an axe slicing through a log.

Kelly Jane cannoned into the bannisters and rebounded onto the top step, breathless and exhilarated. She'd stopped the burglar! She was a hero!

But where were her mum and dad? Surely they couldn't have slept through all of this?

She opened their bedroom door and saw to her dismay that their bed was empty, the curtains still wide open. Where were they? What was going on? And why hadn't anyone sounded the alarm?

Back on the landing, she peered down the stairs and saw a

crumpled heap in the hallway. He wasn't moving. Nervously, she decided she'd better call the police herself.

She inched down the stairs, never taking her eyes off the burglar in case he suddenly jumped up and came after her.

Step by careful step, she edged closer.

Three stairs from the bottom, enough light spilled in through the glass panels in the front door for Kelly Jane to see what she'd really done.

There, in the middle of the hallway, lay the prone body of Santa Claus. Not moving. Not even breathing.

She'd killed Santa Claus.

Simon Sharp was wrong. Sarah was right. And now Kelly Jane had killed him.

With a stifled scream, she turned tail and raced back to her bedroom, slamming the door shut behind her. Now she was shivering in earnest, her whole body trembling from head to foot. She dived into bed, pulling the duvet over her head. But it made no difference. She felt as if her body had turned to stone, her blood to ice. She couldn't stop shaking, her teeth chattering like popcorn in a pan.

She'd killed Santa Claus.

All over the world, children would wake up to no Christmas presents because Kelly Jane Davidson had murdered Santa. And everyone would know whom to blame, because his dead body was lying in her hallway. Until the day she died, people would point at her in the street and go, 'There's Kelly Jane Davidson, the girl who murdered Christmas.'

Whimpering, she lay curled under her duvet, terrible remorse flooding her heart. She'd never sleep again.

But somehow, she did. When her mum threw open the door and shouted 'Merry Christmas!' Kelly Jane was sound asleep. For one wonderful moment, she forgot what had happened. Then it came pouring back in and she peered timidly over the edge of the duvet at her mum. She didn't seem upset or worried. How could she have missed the dead body in the hall?

'Don't you want your presents?' her mum asked. 'I can't believe you're still in bed. It's nine o'clock. You've never slept this late on Christmas morning before. Come on, Santa's been!'

Nobody knew that better than Kelly Jane. What had happened? Had the reindeer summoned the elves to take Santa's body away, leaving her presents behind? Was she going to be the only child who had Christmas presents this year? Reluctantly, she climbed out of bed and dawdled downstairs behind her mum, gazing in worried amazement at the empty expanse of the hall carpet.

She trailed into the living-room, feet dragging with every step. There, under the tree, was the usual pile of brightly wrapped gifts. Kelly Jane looked up at her mum, an anxious frown on her face. 'Are these all for me?' she asked. Somehow, it felt wrong to be rewarded for killing Santa Claus.

Her mum grinned. 'All for you. Oh, and there was a note with them as well.' She handed Kelly Jane a Christmas card with a picture of a reindeer on the front.

Kelly Jane took it gingerly and opened it. Inside, in shaky capital letters, it read, 'Don't worry. You can never kill me. I'm magic. Happy Christmas from Santa Claus.'

A slow smile spread across her face. It was all right! She hadn't murdered Santa after all!

Before she could say another word, the door to the kitchen opened and her dad walked in. He had the biggest black eye Kelly Jane had ever seen, even on the telly. The whole of one side of his face was all bruised, and his left arm was encased in plaster. 'What happened, Dad?' she asked, running to hug him in her dismay.

He winced. 'Careful, Kelly, I'm all bruised.'

'But what happened to you?' she demanded, stepping back.

'Your dad had a bit too much to drink at the office party last night,' her mum said hastily. 'He had a fall.'

'But I'm going to be just fine. Why don't you open your presents?' he said, gently pushing Kelly Jane towards the tree.

As she stripped the paper from the first of her presents, her mum and dad stood watching. 'That'll teach me to leave you alone in the house on Christmas Eve,' her mum said softly.

Her dad tried to smile, but gave up when the pain kicked in. 'Bloody Santa suit,' he said. 'How was I to know she'd take me for a burglar?'

Sneeze for Danger

I shifted in my canvas chair, trying to get uncomfortable. The hardest thing about listening to somebody sleeping is staying awake yourself. Mind you, there wasn't much to hear. Greg Thomas was never going to get complaints from his girlfriends about his snoring. I'd come on stake-out duty at midnight, and all I'd heard was the tinny tail-end of some American sports commentary on the TV, the flushing of a toilet and a few grunts that I took to be him getting comfortable in the big bed that dominated his extravagantly stylish studio penthouse.

I knew about the bed and the expensive style because we also had video surveillance inside Thomas's flat. Well, we'd had it till the previous afternoon. According to Jimmy Lister, who shared the day shift, Thomas had stopped in at the florist's on his way back from a meet with one of his dealers and emerged with two big bunches of lilies. Back at the flat, he'd stuffed them into a vase and placed them right in front of the wee fibre-optic camera. Almost as if he knew.

But of course, he couldn't have known. If he'd had any inkling that we were watching, it wouldn't have been business as usual in the Greg Thomas drugs empire. He wouldn't have gone near his network of middlemen, and he certainly wouldn't have been calling his partner in crime to discuss her forthcoming trip to Curaçao. If he'd known we were watching him, he'd have assumed we were trying to close him down and he'd have been living the blameless life.

He'd have been wrong. I'm not that sort of cop. That's not to say I don't think people like Greg Thomas should be put away for a very long time. They should. They are responsible for a disproportionate amount of human misery, and they don't deserve to be inhabiting the high life. Thomas's cupidity played on others' stupidity, but that didn't make any of it all right.

Nevertheless, my interest was not in making a case against Thomas. What mattered to me was the reason nobody else had been able to do just that. Three times the Drugs Squad had initiated operations against Greg Thomas's multi-million-pound business, and three times they'd come away empty-handed. There was only one possible conclusion. Somebody on the inside was taking Thomas's shilling.

Samuels, who runs the drugs squad, had finally conceded he wasn't going to put Greg Thomas away until he'd put his own house in order. And that's where we came in.

Nobody loves us. Our fellow cops call us the Scaffies. That's Scots for bin men. My brother, who studied Scottish literature at university, says it's probably a corruption of scavengers. Me, I prefer to knock off the first two letters. Avengers, that's what we are. We're there to avenge the punters who pay our wages and get robbed of justice because some cops see get-rich-quick opportunities where the rest of us see the chance to make a collar.

It's easy to be cynical in my line of work. When your job is to sniff out corruption, it's hard to see past that. It's difficult to hang on to the missionary zeal when you're constantly exposed to the venality of your fellow man. I've seen cops selling their mates down the river for the price of a package holiday. Sometimes I almost believe that some of them do it for the same reason as criminals commit crimes – because they can. And they're the ones who are most affronted when we sit them down and confront them with what they've done.

So. Nobody loves us. But what's worse is that doing this job for any length of time provokes a kind of emotional reversal. It's almost impossible for us Scaffies to love anybody. Mistrust becomes a habit and nothing will poison a relationship faster than that. In the end, all you've got is your team. There's eight of us, and we're closer than most marriages. We're a detective inspector, two sergeants and five constables. But rank matters less here than anywhere else in the force. We need to believe in each other, and that's the bottom line.

Movement in the street below caught my attention. A shambling figure, staggering slightly, making his way down the pavement opposite our vantage point. I nudged my partner Dennis, who rolled his shoulders as he leaned forward, focused the camera and snapped off a couple of shots. Not that they'd be any use. The three a.m. drunk was dressed for the weather, the collar of his puffa jacket close round his neck and his baseball cap pulled down low. He stopped outside Thomas's building and keyed the entry code into the door. There were sixteen flats in the block and we knew most of the residents by sight. I didn't recognise this guy, though.

Through the glass frontage of the building opposite, we could see him weaving his way to the lift. He hit the call button and practically fell inside when the doors opened. I was fully alert now. Not because I thought anything untoward was going down, but because anything that gets the adrenaline going in the middle of night surveillance is welcome. The lift stopped on the second floor, and the drunk lurched out into the lobby, turning to his left and heading for one of the flats at the rear of the building.

We relaxed and settled back into our chairs. Dennis, my partner, snorted. 'I wouldn't like to be inside his head in the morning,' he said.

I reached down and pulled a thermos of coffee out of my bag. 'You want some?'

Dennis shook his head. 'I'll stick to the Diet Coke,' he said.

It was about fifteen minutes later that we heard it. Our headphones exploded into life with a volley of sneezing. I nearly fell out of my chair. The volume was deafening. It seemed to go on forever. A choking, spluttering, gasping fit that I thought would never end. Then, as suddenly as it had started, it ended. I looked at Dennis. 'What the hell was that?'

He shrugged. 'Guy's coming down with a cold?'

'Out of the blue? Just like that?'

'Maybe he decided to have a wee taste of his own product.'

'Oh aye, right. You wake up in the night, you can't get back to sleep, so you do a line of coke?'

Dennis laughed. 'Right enough,' he said.

We left it at that. After all, there's nothing inherently suspicious about somebody having a sneezing fit in the middle of the night. Unless, of course, they never wake up.

I was spark out myself when Greg Thomas made his presence felt again. Groggy with tiredness, I reached for the phone, registering the time on my bedside clock. Just after one o'clock. I'd been in bed for less than four hours. I'd barely grunted a greeting when a familiar voice battered my eardrum.

'What the hell were you doing last night?' Detective Inspector Phil Barclay demanded.

'Listening in, boss,' I said. 'With Dennis. Like I was supposed to be. Why?'

'Because while you were listening in, somebody cut Greg Thomas's throat.'

On my way to the scene, I called Jimmy Lister and tried to piece together what had happened. When the dayshift hadn't heard a peep out of Thomas by noon, they'd grown suspicious. They began to wonder if he'd somehow done a runner. So they'd got the management company to let them into Thomas's flat and they'd found him sprawled across his bed, throat gaping like some monstrous grin.

By the time I got to the flat, there was a huddle of people on the landing. Drugs Squad, Serious Crime guys and of course, the Scaffies. Phil Barclay was at the centre of the group. 'There you are, Chrissie,' he said. 'So how the hell did you miss a murder while you were staking out the victim?' For Phil to turn on one of his own in front of other cops was unheard of. I knew I was in for a very rough ride.

Before I could answer, Dennis emerged from the stairwell. 'Listen to the tapes, boss,' he said. 'Then you'll hear everything *we* did. Which is nothing.'

'Except for the sneezing,' I said slowly.

All the eyes were on me now. 'About twenty past three. Somebody had a sneezing fit. It must have lasted a couple of minutes at least.' I looked at Dennis, who nodded in confirmation.

'We assumed it was Thomas,' he said.

'That would fit,' one of the other cops said. I didn't know his name, but I knew he was Serious Crime. 'The pathologist estimates time of death between two and five a.m.'

Samuels from the Drugs Squad stuck his head out of the flat. 'Phil, do you want to take a look inside, see if anything's out of place from when you had the video running?'

Barclay looked momentarily uncomfortable. 'Chrissie, you and Dennis take a look. I didn't really pay much attention to the video footage.'

'Talk about distancing yourself,' Dennis muttered as we entered the flat, sidestepping a SOCO who was examining the lock on the door through a jeweller's loupe.

I paused and said, 'Key or picks?'

The SOCO looked up. 'Picks, I'd say. Fresh scratches on the tumblers.'

'He must have been bloody good,' I said. 'We never heard a thing.'

Greg Thomas wasn't a pretty sight. I was supposed to be looking round the flat, but my eyes were constantly drawn back to the bed. 'How come we never heard it? You'd think he'd have made some sort of noise.'

One of the technicians looked up from the surface he was dusting for prints. 'The doc said it must have been an incredibly sharp blade. Went through right to the spine, knife through butter. He maybe would have made a wee gurgle, but that's all.'

At first glance, nothing in the flat looked different. I stepped round the bed towards the alcove where Thomas had his workstation. 'His laptop's gone,' I said, pointing to the cable lying disconnected on the desk.

'Great. So now we know we're looking for a killer with a laptop,' Dennis said. 'That'll narrow it down.'

Back on the landing, Phil told us abruptly to head back to base. 'We'll have a debrief in an hour,' he said. 'The Drugs Squad guys can run us through Thomas's known associates and enemies. Maybe they'll recognise somebody from our surveillance.'

I walked back to my car, turning everything over in my head. The timing stuck in my throat. It felt like an uncomfortable coincidence that Greg Thomas had been killed the very night we'd lost our video cover. I knew Phil Barclay and Samuels were tight from way back and wondered whether my boss had mentioned the problem to Samuels. If the mole knew we were watching, he might have decided the best way to avoid detection was to silence his paymaster for good. That would also explain the silence. None of Thomas's rivals could have known about the need to keep the noise levels down.

Slowly, an idea began to form in my head. We might have lost the direct route to the Drugs Squad's bad apple, but maybe there was still an indirect passage to the truth. I made a wee detour on the way back to the office, wondering at my own temerity for even daring to think the way I was.

The debrief was the usual mixture of knowledge and speculation, but because there were three separate teams involved, the atmosphere was edgy. The DI from the Crime Squad told us to assume our unidentified drunk was the killer. He hadn't been heading for a flat, he'd been making for the back stairs. Apparently the lock on the door leading to the penthouse floor showed signs of having been forced. He'd probably left by the same route, using the fire door at the rear of the building. He showed our pix on the big screen but not even the guy's mother could have identified him from that. 'And that is all we know so far,' he said.

The silhouette I'd been expecting finally showed up outside the frosted glass door of the briefing room. I put up my hand. 'Not quite all, sir,' I said. 'We also know he's allergic to lily pollen.'

As I spoke, the door opened and the desk officer walked in, looking sheepish behind a big bouquet of stargazer lilies. The fragrance spread out in an arc before him as he walked towards Samuels. 'I was told these were urgent,' he said apologetically.

I held my breath, my eyes nailed to the astonished faces of Samuels and his cohort of Drugs Squad detectives.

And that's when Phil Barclay shattered the stunned silence with a fusillade of sneezes.

Guilt Trip

As neither of my parents was too bothered about religion, I managed to miss out on Catholic guilt. Then I found myself working with Shelley. A guilt trip on legs, our office manager. If she treats her two teenagers like she treats me, those kids are going to be in therapy for years. 'You play, you pay,' she said sweetly, pushing the new case file towards me for the third time.

'Just because I play computer games doesn't mean I'm qualified to deal with the nerds who write them,' I protested. It was only a white lie; although my business partner Bill Mortensen deals with most of the work we do involving computers, I'm not exactly a techno-illiterate. I pushed the file back towards Shelley. 'It's one for Bill.'

'Bill's too busy. You know that,' Shelley said. 'Anyway, it's not software as such. It's either piracy or industrial sabotage and that's your forte.' The file slid back to me.

'Sealsoft are Bill's clients.' Brannigan's last stand.

'All the more reason you should get to know them.'

I gave in and picked up the file. Shelley gave a tight little smile and turned back to her computer screen. One of these days I'm going to get the last word. Just wait till hell freezes over, that's all. Just wait. On my way out of the door and down the stairs, I browsed the file. Sealsoft was a local Manchester games software house. They'd started off back in the dawn of computer gaming in the mid-eighties, writing programs for a whole range of hardware. Some of the machines they produced games for had never been intended as anything other than word processors, but Sealsoft had grabbed the challenge and come up with some fun stuff. The first platform game I'd ever played, on a word processor that now looked as antique as a Model-T Ford, had been a Sealsoft game.

They'd never grown to rival any of the big players in the field, but somehow Sealsoft had always hung in there, coming up every now and again with seemingly simple games that became classics. In the last year or two they'd managed to win the odd film tie-in licence, and their latest acquisition was the new Arnold Schwarzenegger and Bruce Willis boys 'n' toys epic. But now, two weeks before the game was launched, they had a problem. And when people have problems, Mortensen and Brannigan is where they turn if they've got sense and cash enough.

I had a ten o'clock appointment with Sealsoft's boss. Luckily I could get there on foot, since parking round by Sealsoft is a game for the terminally reckless. The company had started off on the top floor of a virtually derelict canal-side warehouse that has since been gutted and turned into expansive and expensive studio flats where the marginally criminal rub shoulders with the marginally legitimate lads from the financial services industries. Sealsoft had moved into modern premises a couple of streets away from the canal, but the towpath was still the quickest way to get from my office in Oxford Road to their concrete pillbox in Castlefield.

Fintan O'Donohoe had milk-white skin and freckles so pale it looked like he'd last seen daylight somewhere in the nineteenth century. He looked about seventeen, which was slightly worrying since I knew he'd been with the company since it started up in 1983. Add that to the red-rimmed eyes and I felt like I'd stumbled into *Interview with the Vampire*. We settled in his chrome and black-leather office, each of us clutching our designer combinations of mineral water, herbs and juices.

'Call me Fin,' he said, with no trace of any accent other than pure Mancunian.

I resisted the invitation. It wasn't the hardest thing I'd done that day. 'I'm told you have a problem,' I said.

'That's not the word I'd use,' he sighed. 'A major disaster waiting to happen is what we've got. We've got a boss money-earner about to hit the streets and suddenly our whole operation's under threat.'

'From what?'

'It started about six weeks ago. There were just one or two at first, but we've had getting on for sixty in the last two days. It's a nightmare,' O'Donohoe told me earnestly, leaning forward and fiddling anxiously with a pencil.

'What exactly are we talking about here?' He might not have anything better to do than take a long tour round the houses, but I certainly did. Apart from anything else, there was a cappuccino at the Atlas café with my name on it.

'Copies of our games with the right packaging, the right manuals, the guarantee cards, everything, are being returned to us because the people who buy them are shoving the disks into their computers and finding they're completely blank. Nothing on them at all. Just bog-standard high-density pre-formatted unbranded three-and-a-half-inch disks.' He threw himself back in his chair, pouting like a five year old.

'Sounds like pirates,' I said. 'Bunch of schneid merchants copying your packaging and stuffing any old shit in there.'

He shook his head. 'My first thought. But that's not how the pirates work. They bust your copy protection codes, make hundreds of copies of the program and stick it inside pretty crudely copied packaging. This is the opposite of that. There's no game, but the packaging is perfect. It's ours.' He opened a drawer in his desk and pulled out a box measuring about eight inches by ten and a couple of inches deep. The cover showed an orc and a human in mortal combat outlined in embossed silver foil. O'Donohoe opened the box and tipped out a game manual, a story book, four disks with labels reading 1–4 and guarantee card. 'Right down to the hologram seal on the guarantee, look,' he pointed out.

I leaned forward and picked up the card, turning it to check the hologram. He was right; if this was piracy, I'd never seen quality like it. And if they could produce packaging this good, I was damn sure they could have copied the game too. So why the combination of spot-on packaging and blank disks? 'Weird,' I said.

'You're not kidding.'

'Is this happening to any of your competitors?'

'Not that I've heard. And I would have heard, I think.'

Sounded as if one of Sealsoft's rivals was paying off an insider to screw O'Donohoe's operation into the deck. 'Where are the punters buying them? Market stalls?' I asked.

Head down, O'Donohoe said, 'Nope.' For the first time I noted the dark shadows under his eyes. 'They're mostly coming back to us via the retailers, though some are coming direct.'

'Which retailers? Independents or chains?' I was sitting

forward in my seat now, intrigued. What had sounded like a boring piece of routine was getting more interesting by the minute. Call me shallow and superficial, but I like a bit of excitement in my day.

'Mostly smallish independents, but increasingly we're getting returns from the big chain stores now. We've been in touch with quite a few of the customers as well, and they're all saying that the games were shrink-wrapped when they bought them.'

I sat back, disappointed. The shrink-wrapping was the clincher.

'It's an inside job,' I said flatly. 'Industrial sabotage.'

'No way,' O'Donohoe said, two pale pink spots suddenly burning on his cheekbones.

'I'm sorry. I know it's the message no employer wants to hear. But it's clearly an inside job.'

'It can't be,' he insisted bluntly. 'Look, I'm not a dummy. I've been in this game a while. I know the wrinkles. I know how piracy happens. And I guard against it. Our boxes are printed in one place, our booklets in another, our guarantee cards in a third. The disks get copied in-house onto disks that are overprinted with our logo and the name of the game, so you couldn't just slip in a few blanks like these,' he said contemptuously, throwing the disks across the desk.

'Where does it all come together?' I asked.

'We're a small company,' he answered obliquely. 'But that's not the only reason we pack by hand rather than on a production line. I know where we're vulnerable to sabotage, and I've covered the bases. The boxes are packed and sealed in shrink-wrap in a room behind the despatch room.'

'Then that's where your saboteur is.'

His lip curled. 'I don't think so. I've only got two workers in there. We've always had a policy of employing friends and family at Sealsoft. The packers are my mum and her sister, my Auntie Geraldine. They'd kill anybody that was trying to sabotage this business, take my word for it. When they're not working, the door's double-locked. They wouldn't even let the parish priest in there, believe me.'

'So what exactly do you want me to do?' I asked.

'I don't want you questioning my staff,' he said irritably. 'Other than that, it's up to you. You're the detective. Find out who's putting the shaft in, then come back and tell me.'

When I left Sealsoft ten minutes later, all I had to go on was a list of customers and companies involved in returns of Sealsoft's games, and details of who'd sent back what. I was still pretty sure the villain was inside the walls rather than outside, but the client wasn't letting me anywhere near his good Catholic mother and Auntie Geraldine. Can't say I blamed him.

I figured there wasn't a lot of point in starting with the chain stores. Even if something hooky was going on, they were the last people I could lean on to find out. With dole queues still well into seven figures, the staff there weren't going to tell me anything that might cost them their jobs. I sat in the Atlas over the coffee I'd promised myself and read through the names. At first glance, I didn't recognise any of the computer-game suppliers. We buy all our equipment and consumables by mail order, and the only shop we've ever used in dire emergencies was the one that used to occupy the ground floor of our building before it became a supermarket.

Time for some expert help. I pulled out my mobile and rang my tame darkside hacker, Gizmo. By day he works for

Telecom as a systems manager. By night, he becomes the Scarlet Pimpernel of cyberspace. Or so he tells me. 'Giz? Kate.'

'Not a secure line,' he grumbled. 'You should know better.'

'Not a problem. This isn't top secret. Do you know anybody who works at any of these outlets?' I started to read out the list, Gizmo grunting negatively after each name. About halfway through the list, he stopped me.

'Wait a minute. That last one, Epic PC?'

'You know someone there?'

'I don't but you do. It's wossname, the geezer that used to have that place under your office.'

'Deke? He went bust, didn't he?'

''S right. Bombed. Went into liquidation, opened up a new place in Prestwich Village a week later, didn't he? That's his shop. Epic PC. I remember because I thought it was such a crap name. That everything?'

'That'll do nicely, Giz.' I was speaking to empty air. I like a man who doesn't waste my time. I drained my cup, walked up the steps to Deansgate station and jumped on the next tram to Prestwich.

Epic PC was a small shop on the main drag. I recognised the special offer stickers. It looked like Deke Harper didn't have the kind of fresh ideas that would save Epic PC from its predecessor's fate. I pushed open the door and an electric buzzer vibrated in the stuffy air. Deke himself was seated behind a PC in the middle of a long room that was stuffed with hardware and software, his fingers clattering over the keys. He'd trained himself well in the art of looking busy; he let a whole five seconds pass between the buzzer sounding and his eyes leaving the screen in front of him. When he registered who his customer was, his eyebrows climbed in his narrow face. 'Hello,' he said uncertainly, pushing his chair back and getting to his feet. 'Stranger.'

'Believe me, Deke, it gets a lot stranger still,' I said drily.

'I didn't know you lived out this way,' he said nervously, hitting a key to clear his screen as I drew level with him.

'I don't,' I said. Sometimes it's just more fun to let them come to you.

'You were passing?'

'No.' I leaned against his desk. His eyes kept flickering between me and his uninformative screen.

'You needed something for the computer? Some disks?'

'Three in a row, Deke. You lose. My turn now. I'm here about these moody computer games you've been selling. Where are they coming from?'

A thin blue vein in his temple seemed to pup up from nowhere. 'I don't know what you're on about,' he said, too nonchalantly. 'What moody computer games?'

I rattled off half a dozen Sealsoft games. 'I sell them, sure,' he said defensively. 'But they're not hooky. Look, I got invoices for them,' he added, pushing past me and yanking a drawer open. He pulled out a loose-leaf file and flicked through fast enough to rip a couple of pages before he arrived at a clutch of invoices from Sealsoft.

I took the file from him and walked over to the shelves and counted. 'According to this, Deke, you bought six copies of Sheer Fire II when it was released last month.'

'That's right. And there's only five there now, right? I sold one.'

'Wrong. You sold at least three. That's how many of your customers have returned blank copies of Sheer Fire II to

Sealsoft. Care to explain the discrepancy? Or do I have to call your local friendly Trading Standards Officer?' I asked sweetly. 'You can go down for this kind of thing these days, can't you?' I added conversationally.

Half an hour later I was sitting outside Epic PC behind the wheel of Deke's six-year-old Mercedes, waiting for a lad he knew only as Jazbo to turn up in response to a call on his mobile. Amazing what people will do with a little incentive. I spotted Jazbo right away from Deke's description. A shade under six feet, jeans, trainers and a Chicago Cubs bomber jacket. And Tony Blair complains about Manchester United's merchandising. At least they're local.

He got out of a battered boy racer's hatchback, clutching a carrier bag with box-shaped outlines pressing against it. I banged off a couple of snaps with the camera from my backpack. Jazbo was in and out of Epic PC inside five minutes. We headed back into town down Bury New Road, me sitting snugly on his tail with only one car between us. We skirted the city centre and headed east. Jazbo eventually parked up in one of the few remaining terraced streets in Gorton and let himself into one of the houses. I took a note of the address and drove Deke's Merc back to Prestwich before he started getting too twitchy about the idea of me with his wheels.

Next morning, I was back outside Jazbo's house just before seven. Early risers, villains, in my experience. According to the electoral roll, Gladys and Albert Conway lived there. I suspected the information on the list was well out of date. With names like that, they might have been Jazbo's grandparents, but a more likely scenario was that he'd taken over the house after the Conways had died or suffered the fate worse than death of an old people's home. The man himself emerged about five past the hour. There was less traffic around, but I managed to stay in contact with him into the city centre, where he parked in a loading bay behind Deansgate and let himself into the back of the shop.

I took a chance and left my wheels on a single yellow while I walked round the front of the row of shops and counted back to where Jazbo had let himself in. JJ's Butty Bar. Another piece of the jigsaw clicked into place.

Through the window, I caught the occasional glimpse of Jazbo, white-coated, moving between tall fridges and countertops. Once or twice he emerged from the rear of the shop with trays of barm cakes neatly wrapped and labelled, depositing them in the chill cabinets round the shop. I figured he was good for a few hours yet and headed back to the office before the traffic wardens came out to play.

I was back just after two. I kept cruising round the block till someone finally left a meter clear that gave me a clear view of the exit from the alley behind the sandwich shop. Jazbo emerged in his hot hatch just after three, which was just as well because I was running out of change. I stayed close to him through the city centre, then let a bit of distance grow between us as he headed out past Salford Quays and into the industrial estate round Trafford Park. He pulled up outside a small unit with Gingerbread House painted in a rainbow of colours across the front wall. Jazbo disappeared inside.

About fifteen minutes later he emerged with a supermarket trolley filled to the top with computer-game boxes. I was baffled. I'd had my own theory about where the packaging was coming from, and it had just been blown out of the water. I hate being wrong. I'd rather unblock the toilet. I let

Jazbo drive off, then I marched into Gingerbread House. Ten minutes later I had all the answers.

Fintan O'Donohoe looked impressed as I laid out my dossier before him. Jazbo's address, photograph, phone number, car registration and place of work would be more than enough to hand him over to the police, gift-wrapped. 'So how's this guy getting hold of the gear?' he demanded.

'First thing I wondered about was the shrink-wrapping. That made me think it was someone in your despatch unit. But you were adamant it couldn't be either your mum or your auntie. Then when I found out he worked in a sandwich shop, I realised he must be using their wrap-and-seal gear to cover his boxes in. Which left the question of where the boxes were coming from. You ruled out an inside job, so I thought he might simply be raiding your dustbins for discarded gear. But I was wrong. You ever heard of a charity called Gingerbread House?'

O'Donohoe frowned. 'No. Should I have?'

'Your mum has,' I told him. 'And so, I suspect, has Jazbo's mum or girlfriend or sister. It's an educational charity run by nuns. They go round businesses and ask them for any surplus materials and they sell them off to schools and playgroups for next to nothing. They collect all sorts – material scraps, bits of bungee rope, offcuts of specialist paper, wallpaper catalogues, tinsel, sheets of plastic, scrap paper. Anything that could come in handy for schools projects or for costumes for plays, whatever.'

Fintan O'Donohoe groaned and put his hands over his face. 'Don't tell me . . .'

'They came round here a few months ago, and your mum

explained that you don't manufacture here, so there's not much in the way of leftover stuff. But what there was were the boxes from games that had been sent back because they were faulty in some way. The disks were scrapped, and so were the boxes and manuals normally. But if the nuns could make any use of the boxes and their contents . . . Your mum or your Auntie Geraldine's been dropping stuff off once a fortnight ever since.'

He looked up at me, a ghost of an ironic smile on his lips. 'And I was so sure it couldn't be anything to do with my mum!'

'Don't they say charity begins at home?'

Homecoming

Oblivious to any echoes, filmic or literary, Miranda Bryant said that she would buy the flowers herself.

Peter had made the offer sincerely, willing to take on part of the burden of organising their first dinner party in their new city. But he was relieved to have avoided any disruption to a day he would spend with women who paid him large sums of money to change what they saw in the mirror. He knew he did his best work when there was nothing external to distract him.

Miranda knew that too. She liked the rewards his work had brought them and so she'd been content to set her own ambitions to one side. There was no room in their marriage for two high-flying medical careers. Instead of the neuro-surgery she'd once dreamed of performing, she'd specialised in dermatology. Plenty of opportunity for part-time work and no call-outs at night or weekends. Plenty of opportunity to make sure Peter's life ran smoothly.

She stood in her immaculate kitchen and began to organise her purchases. Finest Italian artichokes, char-grilled and marinated in olive oil speckled with fragments of herbs; dark red organic Aberdeen Angus steaks with porphyry marbling of fat; transparent slices of pancetta; broad sage leaves with their curious texture; plump scallops, their vivid corals curled like commas round the succulent white flesh. Beautiful, sensual, ready to fill an emptiness.

She reached for a small, sharp, strong knife and slit open a plastic bag, spilling oysters over the granite worktop. She picked one up, running her thumb over the layered shell. So ugly on the outside, so perfect on the inside, they reminded her of what Peter tried to do with his patients. The thought irritated her and she reached for the radio. '*And this after-noon on* Castaway, *our guest is an international bestselling thriller writer. She's published twenty-three novels, translated into more than thirty languages. She's won awards for her work on three continents, and judging by the quotes on her book jackets, she is the thriller writer's thriller writer. Jane Carson, welcome to Radio Dunedin.*'

'*Thanks, Simon. It's a pleasure to be here.*'

The knife skidded across the uneven ridges of the shell, slicing deep into the base of Miranda's thumb. For a moment, shock immobilised her. The slit of blood swelled fat and spread, running down the ball of her thumb towards the thin white scar on her wrist. 'Damn it to hell,' she said, turning on her heel and hurrying towards the cloakroom where the nearest first aid kit was stowed. She couldn't believe herself. Just as well she'd turned her back on surgery if she couldn't even shuck an oyster without bleeding all over the kitchen.

Miranda cleaned the wound with an antiseptic wipe then efficiently closed it with micropore tape. She walked back to the kitchen, rubbing the tape down firmly. 'Turn off the radio,' she said out loud. But her hand remained poised, halfway to the switch.

'*. . . goes back twenty-five years to when I was an under-graduate at Girton.*'

'*And what's so special about this record, Jane?*'

(a deep, warm chuckle) 'It reminds me of my first great love affair.'

'Was that when you realised you were gay?'

'I'd realised that quite a while before, Simon. But it was the first time I fell in love with a woman who loved me in return. This record reminds me of what that felt like. The intensity, the excitement, the sense of possibility. And of course the desperation and the desolation when it all went horribly wrong.'

'You like to be reminded of how it all went wrong?'

'I'm a writer, Simon. Everything is material.'

'Well, I hate to think what you're going to make of me, Jane!'

'Probably a corpse, Simon.'

(nervous laugh) 'Now you're really worrying me. But let's have your first record. It's Joan Armatrading's "Love and Affection".'

The opening notes filled the kitchen, transporting Miranda back to her own youth. She tried to fight it, reminding herself of Noël Coward's sardonic dictum about the potency of cheap music. But memory was in command now, undeniable. She could feel the thin warmth of spring sunshine, the faint damp of the grass penetrating her clothes, the heat in her skin like fever. Dark against the eggshell blue of the sky, a profile leaning over her, lips parted, jawline taut. Then the sun blotted out by the first kiss. She'd thought she understood desire, but had immediately comprehended her mistake.

Nothing had prepared her for that moment, or for what followed. Everything that had gone before seemed small, quiet, colourless. Love had hit her with an amplification of the senses that left her feeling unpeeled. Where her lover rejoiced in the awakening, Miranda fretted over what it might mean.

They never articulated it to each other, but each was conscious that they didn't want to share whatever was happening between them with the rest of the world. It demanded discretion. They met behind the closed doors of their own rooms or else privately in public places. At prearranged times in libraries, apparently by chance on walks by the river, seemingly happenstance attendances at the same parties which they studiously left separately. Their private names for each other echoed their love of secrecy. Miranda was Orlando – Virginia Woolf had been iconic then – and her beloved, The Kid, for reasons more obvious to anyone twenty or thirty years their senior. Not only did this make them feel they had created each other afresh, it also meant that any curious friend picking up a card or note would be none the wiser.

Miranda loved it when they went to the cinema or the theatre. Not that she was particularly interested in film or drama; even then, she had had little interest in the fictive world, preferring the hard edges of science and philosophy. What she loved was the gradual descent into darkness, when The Kid's hand would creep across her thigh and enclose her fingers. Even more, she loved the opportunity secretly to study The Kid, too absorbed in whatever was unfolding to sense Miranda's scrutiny. Even now, as the dying strains of Armatrading's voice faded on the radio, Miranda could picture that intent profile, lips slightly parted as if ready for the next kiss. Watching The Kid in the variable dark, now there was joy.

'It's a time machine, music like that.'

'You're so right, Jane. It recreates the memories any castaways would want to take with them to a desert island. Now,

after Cambridge, you went to America to do a postgraduate degree in creative writing, didn't you? Why America?'

'Back then, there weren't many creative writing courses here in the UK. And I also wanted to put as much distance between me and Cambridge as I could.'

Miranda too suddenly wanted some distance. She hurried across the kitchen to the French doors that led to her court-yard garden. Fresh herbs, that's what she needed. The sharp darkness of rosemary, the bright fragrance of basil, the creeping insistence of thyme. The herbs of her married life.

For almost twenty years, Miranda and Peter had basked in sunshine in Cape Town, their lives gilded with security and success. But latterly, they had both felt drawn back to the cooler climate of their youth. Living in exile was all very well, but the soul eventually craved more familiar tastes and smells. Miranda knew she pined for something, and thought it was home. Edinburgh had seemed like the answer.

Their first two months had kept her too busy to test the hypothesis. Moving into a new home, buying furniture and art, discovering the best restaurants, trying to assimilate twenty years of missed cultural life, negotiating a life without servants; it had challenged Miranda and invigorated her. But there had been no space for reflection.

And now it was upon her, memory's insistence could not be eluded so easily. There was, there could have been, nothing predictable or assumed about the pattern of their love. It was up to them to make it up as they went along, and The Kid was never short of invention. The Kid loved to play games. One week, they'd decided to eat nothing but white food. The challenge had been to make it exciting. They'd started with the obvious; white bread, cottage cheese, natural yoghurt. Miranda had thought she'd done well with vanilla ice cream till The Kid pointed out that college kitchens had no freezers and they'd have to eat it all at one sitting. And then, with a huge grin, had proposed how they might make that more interesting . . . Miranda blushed at the memory, her skin tingling. The Kid had also won the contest, with a meal that had seemed impossibly exotic in 1978 – prawn crackers, white asparagus and a Boursin. So much more exoticism than Miranda's tightly conformist background could ever have accommodated. No wonder her mother had hated The Kid on first sight.

Miranda snipped the herbs, lifting them to her face and inhaling deeply. She wanted to banish the distant past, replace it with more recent memories, recollections that would anchor her to the life she had now rather than the life she might have lived. She deliberately turned her thoughts to her dinner party and their guests. An advocate and her banker husband. A medical insurance executive and his girlfriend who did something with a charity for disabled children. One of Peter's colleagues and his wife. Who was, it appeared, nothing more than that. Unbidden and unwanted, Miranda thought how The Kid would have jeered at such a line-up. 'Cheap,' she muttered, walking back into the kitchen.

'So what made you turn to the crime thriller instead of the literary novel you'd studied in America?'

(a dark chuckle) 'The desire for revenge, Simon. There were people I wanted to murder but I knew I'd never get away with it. So I decided to kill them on the page instead.'

'That's pretty scary, Jane. Why on earth did you want to murder them?'

'Because I blamed them for breaking my heart.'

'You wanted to murder your girlfriend?'

'No. I wanted to murder the people who broke us up and nearly destroyed her in the process. But in a way, that's irrelevant. What motivates writers is almost always irrelevant. It's what we do with it in the crucible of imagination that matters. We transform our pain and our frustration into something unrecognisable.'

'So if these people you wanted to murder were to read your books, they wouldn't recognise themselves?'

'Not only would they not recognise themselves, Simon, they wouldn't recognise the situation. What appears on the page seldom has any visible connection to the event that triggered the writer's response.'

'That's amazing, Jane. Now, your next record is Bach's sixth Brandenburg Concerto. Can you tell us why you've chosen it?'

'Two reasons, really. I first discovered Bach when I was at Cambridge, so like the Joan Armatrading, it also takes me back in time. But perhaps more importantly, it's a canon. It revolves around itself, it reinvents itself. It's complex, and it's perfectly structured. In its beginning is its end. And that's exactly how the plot of a thriller should be. You could say that by introducing me to Bach, my first girlfriend also taught me how to plot. It's a lesson . . .'

This time, Miranda's hand reached the switch and clicked the radio off in mid-sentence. While the beef was marinading, she could buy the flowers. She walked up the hill, wondering yet again how Queen Street Gardens stayed green under the blanket of traffic fumes that choked the city centre. It was a relief to enter the fragrance of the florist's. She drank in the heady scents and the underlying aroma of humus as she checked out the array of blooms. Among the mundane domestic chrysanths and carnations were flowers that were exotic for Scotland but which provoked a sharp stab of nostalgia in Miranda. So many mornings she'd sat on her verandah looking out at those very flowers growing in her own African garden. Things had been easier there; there had been nothing to provoke such ambushes of memory as she'd endured that afternoon.

She made a mental list of what she wanted then wove her way past the aluminium buckets to the counter at the back of the shop. As she approached, the low background mutter resolved itself into Radio Dunedin and Miranda faltered.

'Jane, it's been a pleasure having you here this afternoon.'

'Even if I do turn you into a corpse?'

'I suppose that's better than being ignored. My guest this afternoon has been thriller writer Jane Carson, who's appearing tonight at the Assembly Rooms here in Edinburgh at seven o'clock. She'll be reading from her latest novel, The Last Siberian Tiger, *and I can promise you a real thrill.'*

The florist gave Miranda an inquiring look. 'Can I help you?'

Miranda cleared her throat and pointed to a bucket of yellow calla lilies. 'I'd like a dozen of those,' she said.

The florist nodded and made for the bucket. 'They're lovely, aren't they?'

'Yes. I'll have three of the strelizia too. And a couple of bunches of alstromeria.'

Back home, Miranda carefully arranged the flowers in the elegant crystal vases she'd chosen for the dining-room. Like a sleepwalker, she prepared the food, every movement precise and ordered. She checked the white Burgundy was sufficiently chilled and decanted the red to allow it to breathe. Everything was perfect. Everything was ready. This was her life. This was what the world expected of her. Always had. And she had almost always delivered.

Her fingers strayed to the scar on the opposite wrist. She checked the clock. Half past six. Peter would be home at any minute. Guests at seven for seven thirty. The opening movement of Bach's sixth Brandenburg Concerto circled her brain like a tightening noose.

Miranda Bryant took a last look round her perfect kitchen and reached for her coat. She opened her front door and walked out into the Edinburgh evening.

Heartburn

Everybody remarked on how calm I was on Bonfire Night. 'Considering her husband's just run off with another woman, she's very calm,' I overheard Joan Winstanley from the news-agent's say as I persuaded people to buy the bonfire toffee. But it seemed to me that Derek's departure was no reason to miss the annual cricket-club firework party. Besides, I've been in charge of the toffee-selling now for more years than I care to remember, and I'd be reluctant to hand it over to someone else.

So I put a brave face on it and turned up as usual at Mrs Fletcher's at half past five to pick up the toffee, neatly bagged up in quarter-pound lots. I don't know how she does it, given that the pieces are all such irregular shapes and sizes, but the bags all contain the correct weight. I know, because the second year I was in charge of the toffee, I surreptitiously took the bags home and weighed them. I wasn't prepared to be responsible for selling short weight.

Of course, the jungle drums had been beating. Oswald-twistle is a small town, after all. Strange to think that's what drew Derek and me here all those years ago, willing refugees from the inner-city problems of Manchester. Anyway, Mrs Fletcher greeted me with, 'I hear he's gone off.'

Shamefaced, I nodded. 'He did finish building the bonfire before he left,' I added timidly.

'She's always been no better than she should be, that

Janice Duckworth. Of course, your Derek's not the first she's led astray. Though she's never actually gone off with any of them before. That does surprise me. Always liked having her cake and eating it, has Janice.'

I tried to ignore Mrs Fletcher's remarks, but they burned inside me like the scarlet and yellow flames of the makeshift bonfire I'd already passed on the churned-up mud of the rec at the end of her street. I grabbed the toffee ungraciously, and got out as soon as I could.

I drove through the narrow terraced streets rather too fast, something I'm not particularly given to. All around me, the crump and flash of fireworks gave a shocking life to the evening. Rocket trails showered their sparks across the sky like a sudden rash of comets, all predicting the end of the world. Except that the end of my world had come the night before.

Constructing the bonfire had always taken a lot of Derek's time in the weeks leading up to the cricket-club fireworks party. As a civil engineer, he prided himself on its elaborate design and execution. The secret, he told me so often I could recite it from memory, the secret is to build from the middle outwards.

To achieve the perfect bonfire, according to Derek, it was necessary first to construct what looked like a little hut at the heart of the fire. Derek usually made this from planks the thickness of floorboards. The first couple of years I accompanied him, so I speak from the experience of having seen it as well as having heard the lecture on countless occasions. To me, Derek's central structure looked like nothing so much as a primitive outside lavatory.

Round the 'hut', Derek would then build an elaborate construction of wood, cardboard, chipboard, old furniture and anything else that seemed combustible. But the key to his success was that he left a tunnel through the shell of the bonfire that led to the hut.

The night before the bonfire was lit, late in the evening, after all the local hooligans could reasonably be expected to be abed, Derek would enter the tunnel, crawl to the heart of his construction and fill the hut with a mixture of old newspapers and petrol-soaked rags in plastic bags.

Then he would crawl out, back-filling the tunnel behind him with more highly flammable materials. The point at which the tunnel ended, on the perimeter of the bonfire, was where it had to be lit for maximum effect, burning high and bright for hours.

There are doubtless those who think it highly irresponsible to leave the bonfire in so vulnerable a condition overnight, but the cricket club is pretty secure, with a high fence that no one would dream of trying to scale, since it's overlooked by the police station. Besides, because the bonfire was the responsibility of adults, it never became a target for the kind of childish gang rivalry that leads to bonfires being set alight in advance of the scheduled event.

Anyway, this year as usual, Derek went off the night before the fireworks party to put the finishing touches to his monument, carrying the flask of hot coffee laced with brandy which I always provided to help combat the raw November weather. When he hadn't come home by midnight, naturally I was concerned. My first thought was that he'd had some sort of problem with the bonfire. Perhaps a heavy piece of wood had fallen on him, pinning him to the ground. I drove down to the cricket ground, but it was deserted. The bonfire was finished, though. I checked.

I went home and paced the floor for a while, then I rang the police. Sergeant Mills was very sympathetic, understanding that Derek was not a man to stay out till the small hours except when attending one of those masculine events that involve consuming huge amounts of alcohol and telling the sort of stories we women are supposed to be too sensitive to hear. If he'd been invited back to a fellow member of the fireworks party committee's home for a nightcap, he would have rung me to let me know. He knows how I worry if he's more than a few minutes later than he's told me he'd be. But of course, there was nothing the police could do. Derek is a grown man, after all, and the law allows grown men to stay out all night, if they so desire.

I called Sergeant Mills again the following morning, explaining that there seemed to be no reason to worry, at least not for the police, since, on searching Derek's office for clues, I had uncovered several notes from Janice Duckworth, indicating that they were having an affair and that she wanted them to run away together. It appeared that Derek had been using the bonfire-building as an excuse for seeing more of Janice. I had rung Janice's home, and ascertained from her husband Vic that she too had not returned home from an evening out, supposedly with the girls.

The case seemed cut and dried, as far as Sergeant Mills was concerned. It was humiliating and galling for me, of course, but these things do happen, especially, the sergeant seemed to hint, where middle-aged men and younger blondes are concerned.

* * *

I sold out more quickly than usual this year. I suspect the nosey parkers were seeking me out 'to see how I was taking it' rather than waiting for me to come round to them. Seven o'clock rolled round, and the bonfire was duly lit. It was a particularly spectacular effort this year. Though I grudge admitting it, no one built a bonfire quite like Derek.

I don't suppose he thought when he was building this year's that it would be a funeral pyre for him and Janice Duckworth. He really should have thought of somewhere more romantic for their assignations than a makeshift wooden hut in the middle of a bonfire.

Four Calling Birds

NOREEN

You want to know who to blame for what happened last Wednesday night down at the Roxette? Margaret Thatcher, that's who. Never mind the ones that actually did it. If the finger points at anybody, it should point straight at the Iron Lady. Even though her own body's turned against her now and silenced her, nobody should let pity stand in the way of holding her to account. She made whole communities despair, and when the weak are desperate, sometimes crime seems the easiest way out. Our Dickson says that's an argument that would never stand up in a court of law. But given how useless the police round here are, it's not likely to come to that.

You want to know why what happened last Wednesday night at the Roxette happened at all? You have to go back twenty years. To the miners' strike. They teach it to the bairns now as history, but I lived through it and it's as sharp in my memory as yesterday. After she beat the Argies in the Falklands, Thatcher fell in love with the taste of victory, and the miners were her number-one target. She was determined to break us, and she didn't care what it took. Arthur Scargill, the miners' leader, was as bloody-minded as she was, and when he called his men out on strike, my Alan walked out along with every other miner in his pit.

We all thought it would be over in a matter of weeks at the most. But no bugger would give an inch. Weeks turned into months, the seasons slipped from spring through summer and autumn into winter. We had four bairns to feed and not a penny coming in. Our savings went; then our insurance policies; and finally, my jewellery. We'd go to bed hungry and wake up the same way, our bellies rumbling like the slow grumble of the armoured police vans that regularly rolled round the streets of our town to remind us who we were fighting. Sometimes they'd taunt us by sitting in their vans flaunting their takeaways, even throwing half-eaten fish suppers out on the pavements as they drove by. Anything to rub our noses in the overtime they were coining by keeping us in our places.

We were desperate. I heard tell that some of the wives even went on the game, taking a bus down to the big cities for the day. But nobody from round our way sank that low. Or not that I know of. But lives changed forever during that long hellish year, mine among them.

It's a measure of how low we all sank that when I heard Mattie Barnard had taken a heart attack and died, my first thought wasn't for his widow. It was for his job. I think I got down the Roxette faster than the Co-op Funeral Service got to Mattie's. Tyson Herbert, the manager, hadn't even heard the news. But I didn't let that stop me. 'I want Mattie's job,' I told him straight out while he was still reeling from the shock.

'Now hang on a minute, Noreen,' he said warily. He was always cautious, was Tyson Herbert. You could lose the will to live waiting for him to turn right at a junction. 'You know as well as I do that bingo calling is a man's job. It's always been that way. A touch of authority. Dickie bow and dinner jacket. The BBC might have let their standards slip, but here at the Roxette, we do things the right way.' Ponderous as a bloody elephant.

'That's against the law nowadays, Tyson,' I said. 'You cannot have rules like that any more. Only if you're a lavatory cleaner or something. And as far as I'm aware, cleaning the gents wasn't part of Mattie's job.'

Well, we had a bit of a to and fro, but in the end, Tyson Herbert gave in. He didn't have a lot of choice. The first session of the day was due to start in half an hour, and he needed somebody up there doing two fat ladies and Maggie's den. Even if the person in question was wearing a blue nylon overall instead of a tuxedo.

And that was the start of it all. Now, nobody's ever accused me of being greedy, and besides, I still had a house to run as well as doing my share on the picket line with the other miners' wives. So within a couple of weeks, I'd persuaded Tyson Herbert that he needed to move with the times and make mine a jobshare. By the end of the month, I was splitting my shifts with Kathy, Liz and Jackie. The four calling birds, my Alan christened us. Morning, afternoon and evening, one or other of us would be up on the stage, mike in one hand, plucking balls out of the air with the other and keeping the flow of patter going. More importantly, we kept our four families going. We kept our kids on the straight and narrow.

It made a bit of a splash locally. There had never been women bingo callers in the North-East before. It had been as much a man's job as cutting coal. The local paper wrote an article about us, then the BBC turned up and did an interview with us for *Woman's Hour*. I suppose they were desperate for a story from up our way that wasn't all doom, gloom and picket lines. You should have seen Tyson Herbert preening himself, like he'd single-handedly burned every bra in the North-East.

The fuss soon died down, though the novelty value did bring in a lot of business. Women would come in mini-buses from all around the area just to see the four calling birds. And we carried on with two little ducks and the key to the door like it was second nature. The years trickled past. The bairns grew up and found jobs, which was hard on Alan's pride. He's never worked since they closed the pit the year after the strike. There's no words for what it does to a man when he's dependent on his wife and bairns for the roof over his head and the food on his table.

To tell you the God's honest truth, there were days when it was a relief to get down the Roxette and get to work. We always had a laugh, even in the hardest of times. And there were hard times. When the doctors told Kathy the lump in her breast was going to kill her, we all felt the blow. But when she got too ill to work, we offered her shifts to her Julie. Tyson Herbert made some crack about hereditary peerages, but I told him to keep his nose out and count the takings.

All in all, nobody had any reason for complaint. That is, until Tyson Herbert decided it was time to retire. The bosses at head office didn't consult us about his replacement. Come to that, they didn't consult Tyson either. If they had, we'd never have ended up with Keith Corbett. Keith Cobra, as Julie rechristened him two days into his reign at the Roxette after he tried to grope her at the end of her evening shift.

The nickname suited him. He was a poisonous reptile.

He even looked like a snake, with his narrow wedge of a face and his little dark eyes glittering. When his tongue flicked out to lick his thin lips, you expected it to have a fork at the end. On the third morning, he summoned the four of us to his office like he was God and it was Judgement Day. 'You've had a good run, ladies,' he began, without so much as a cup of tea and a digestive biscuit. 'But things are going to be changing round here. The Roxette is going to be the premier bingo outlet in the area, and that will be reflected in our public image. I'm giving you formal notice of redundancy.'

We were gobsmacked. It was Liz who found her voice first. 'You cannot do that,' she said. 'We've given no grounds for complaint.'

'And how can we be redundant?' I chipped in. 'Somebody has to call the numbers.'

Cobra gave a sly little smile. 'You're being replaced by new technology. A fully automated system. Like on the national lottery. The numbers will go up on a big screen and the computer will announce them.'

We couldn't believe our ears. Replacing us with a machine? 'The customers won't like it,' Julie said.

The Cobra shook his head. 'As long as they get their prizes, they wouldn't care if a talking monkey did the calling. Enjoy your last couple of weeks, ladies.' He turned away from us and started fiddling with his computer.

'You'll regret this,' Liz said defiantly.

'I don't think so,' he said, a sneer on his face. 'Oh, and another thing. This Children in Need night you're planning on Friday? Forget it. The Roxette is a business, not a charity.

Friday night will be just like every other night.'

Well, that did it. We were even more outraged than we were on our own behalf. We'd been doing the Children in Need benefit night for nine years. All the winners donated their prizes, and Tyson Herbert donated a third of the night's takings. It was a big sacrifice all round, but we knew what hardship was, and we all wanted to do our bit.

'You bastard,' Julie said.

The Cobra swung round and glared at her. 'Would you rather be fired for gross misconduct, Julie? Walk out the door with no money and no reference? Because that's exactly what'll happen if you don't keep a civil tongue in your head.'

We hustled Julie out before she could make things worse. We were all fit to be tied, but we couldn't see any way of stopping the Cobra. I broke the news to Alan that teatime. Our Dickson had dropped in too – he's an actor now, he's got a part in one of the soaps, and they'd been doing some location filming locally. I don't know who was more angry, Alan or Dickson. After their tea, the two of them went down to the club full of fighting talk. But I knew it was just talk. There was nothing we could do against the likes of the Cobra.

I was as surprised as anybody when I heard about the armed robbery.

* * *

KEITH

I don't know why I took this job. Everybody knows the Roxette's nothing but trouble. It's never turned the profit it should. And those bloody women. They made Tyson Herbert a laughing stock. But managers' jobs don't come up that often. Plus Head Office said they wanted the Roxette to become one of their flagship venues. And they wanted me to turn it around. Plus Margo's always on at me about Darren needing new this, new that, new the next thing. So how could I say no?

I knew as soon as I walked through the door it was going to be an uphill struggle. There was no sign of the new promo displays that Head Office was pushing throughout the chain. I eventually found them, still in their wrappers, in a cupboard in that pillock Herbert's office. I ask you, how can you drag a business into the twenty-first century if you're dealing with dinosaurs?

And the women. Everywhere, the women. You have to wonder what was going on in Herbert's head. It can't have been that he was dipping his wick, because they were all dogs. Apart from Julie. She was about the only one in the joint who didn't need surgical stockings. Not to mention plastic surgery. I might have considered keeping her on for a bit of light relief between houses. But she made it clear from the off that she had no fucking idea which side her bread was buttered. So she was for the chop like the rest of them.

I didn't hang about. I was right in there, making it clear who was in charge. I got the promo displays up on day one. Then I organised the delivery of the new computerised calling system. And that meant I could give the four calling birds the bullet sooner rather than later. That and knock their stupid charity stunt on the head. I ask you, who throws their profits down the drain like that in this day and age?

By the end of the first week, I was confident that I was all set. I had the decorators booked to bring the Roxette in line with the rest of the chain. Margo was pleased with the extra money in my wage packet, and even Darren had stopped whingeing.

I should have known better. I should have known it was all going too sweet. But not even in my wildest fucking nightmares could I have imagined how bad it could get.

By week two, I had my routines worked out. While the last house was in full swing, I'd do a cash collection from the front of house, the bar and the café. I'd bag it up in the office, ready for the bank in the morning, then put it in the safe overnight. And that's what I was doing on Wednesday night when the office door slammed open.

I looked up sharpish. I admit, I thought it was one of those bloody women come to do my head in. But it wasn't. At first, all I could take in was the barrel of a sawn-off shotgun, pointing straight at me. I nearly pissed myself. Instinctively I reached for the phone but the big fucker behind the gun just growled, 'Fucking leave it.' Then he kicked the door shut.

I dragged my eyes away from the gun and tried to get a look at him. But there wasn't much to see. Big black puffa jacket, jeans, black work boots. Baseball cap pulled down over his eyes, and a ski mask over the rest of his face. 'Keep your fucking mouth shut,' he said. He threw a black sports holdall towards me. 'Fill it up with the cash,' he said.

'I can't,' I said. 'It's in the safe. It's got a time lock.'

'Bollocks,' he said. He waved the gun at me, making me back up against the wall. What happened next was not what I expected. He grabbed the computer keyboard and pulled it across the desk. Then he turned the monitor round so it was facing him. With the hand that wasn't holding the gun, he did a few mouse clicks and then a bit of typing. I tried to edge out of his line of fire, but he wasn't having any. 'Fucking stand still,' he grunted.

Then he turned the screen back to face me and this time I nearly crapped myself. It was a live camera feed from my living-room. Margo and Darren were huddled together on the sofa, eyes wide. Opposite them, his back to the camera, was another big fucker with a shotgun. The picture was a bit fuzzy and wobbly, but there was no mistake about it. Along the bottom of the picture, the seconds ticked away.

'My oppo's only a phone call away. Now are you going to fill the fucking holdall?' he demanded.

Well, I wasn't going to argue, was I? Not with my wife and kid facing a shooter. So I went to the safe. It hasn't got a time lock. Head Office wouldn't spend that kind of money. We're just told to say that to try and put off nutters like the big fucker who was facing me down in my own office. I was sweating so much my fingers were slipping off the keypad. But I managed it at the second go, and a shovelled the bags of cash into his bag as fast as I could.

'Good boy,' he said when I'd finished.

I thought it was all over then. How wrong can you get?

'On your knees,' he ordered me. I didn't know what was going on. Part of me thought he was going to blow me away anyway. I was so fucking scared I could feel the tears in my eyes. I knew I was on the edge of losing it. Of begging him for my life. Only one thing stopped me. I just couldn't believe he was going to kill me. I mean, I know it happens. I know people get topped during robberies. But surely only if they put up a fight? And surely only when the robber is out of control? But this guy was totally calm. He could afford to be – his oppo's gun was still pointing straight at Margo and Darren.

So I fell to my knees.

Just thinking about what came next makes me retch. He dropped the gun to his side, at an angle so the barrel dug right into my gut. Then he unzipped his trousers and pulled out his cock. 'Suck my dick,' he said.

My head jerked back and I stared at him. I couldn't believe what I'd just heard. 'You what?'

'Suck my dick,' he said again, thrusting his hips towards me. His half-hard cock dangled in front of my face. It was the sickest thing I'd ever heard. It wasn't enough for this fucking pervert to terrorise my wife and kid and rob my safe. He wanted me to give him a blow job.

The gun jammed harder into me. 'Just fucking do it,' he said.

So I did.

He grabbed my hair and stopped me pulling back when I gagged. 'That's it. You know you want to,' he said softly, like this was something normal. Which it wasn't, not in any bloody sense.

It felt like it took a lifetime for him to come, but I suppose it was only a few minutes. When I felt his hot load hitting the back of my throat, I nearly bit his cock off in revulsion. But the gun in my chest and the thought of what might happen to Margo and Darren kept me inside the limits.

He stepped back, tucking himself away and zipping up. 'I enjoyed that,' he said.

I couldn't lift my head up. I felt sick to my stomach. And not just from what I'd swallowed either.

'Wait half an hour before you call the cops. We'll be watching, and if there's any funny business, your wife and kid get it. OK?' I nodded. I couldn't speak.

The last thing he did before he left was to help himself to the tape from the video surveillance system that is fed by the camera in my office. In a funny kind of way, I was almost relieved. I didn't want to think about that tape being played in the police station. Or in a courtroom, if it ever came to it.

So I did what I was told. I gave it thirty-five minutes, to be on the safe side. The police arrived like greased lightning. I thought things would get more normal then. Like *The Bill* or something. But it was my night for being well in the wrong. Because that's when things started to get seriously weird.

They'd sent a crew round to the house to check the robbers had kept their word and released Margo and Darren. They radioed back sounding pretty baffled. Turned out Margo was watching the telly and Darren was in his room playing computer games. According to them, that's what they'd been doing all evening. Apart from when Margo had been on the phone to her mate Cheryl. Which had been more or less exactly when I'd supposedly been watching them being held hostage.

That's when the cops started giving me some very fucking funny looks. The boss, a DI Golightly, definitely wasn't living up to his name. 'So how did chummy get in?' he demanded. 'There's no sign of forced entry at the back. And even though they were all eyes down inside the hall, I doubt they would have missed a six foot gunman walking through from the foyer.'

'I don't know,' I said. 'It should all have been locked up. The last person out would have been Liz Kirby. She called the session before the last one.'

By that time, they had the CCTV tapes of the car park. You could see the robber emerge from the shadows on the edge of the car park and walk up to the door. You couldn't see the gun, just the holdall. He opened the door without a moment's hesitation. So that fucking doozy Liz had left it unlocked.

'Looks like he walked straight in,' Golightly said. 'That was lucky for him, wasn't it?'

'I told you. It should have been locked. Look, I'm the victim here.'

He looked me up and down. 'So you say,' he said, sounding like he didn't believe a word of it. Then he wound the tape further back so we could see Liz leaving. And bugger me if she didn't turn round and lock the door behind her. 'How do you explain that?' he said.

All I could do was shrug helplessly.

He kept the digs and insinuations up for a while. He obviously thought there was a chance I was in it up to my eyeballs. But there was fuck all proof so he had to let me go in the end. It was gone four in the morning by the time I got home. Margo was well pissed off. Apparently half the crescent had been glued to their windows after the flashing blue lights had alerted them that there was something more interesting than *Big Brother* going on outside their own front doors. 'I was black affronted,' Margo kept repeating. 'My family's never had the police at their door.' Like mine were a bunch of hardened criminals.

I didn't sleep much. Every time I got near to dropping off, I got flashbacks of that sick bastard's cock. I've never so much as touched another man's dick, not even when I was a kid. I almost wished I'd let the sad sack of shite shoot me.

* * *

DICKSON

Everything I am, I owe to my mam. She taught me that I was as good as anybody else, that there was nothing I couldn't do if I wanted to. She also taught me the meaning of solidarity. Kick one, and we all limp. They should have that on the signs that tell drivers they're entering our town, right below the name of that Westphalian town we're twinned with.

So when she told me and my da what that prize prick Keith Corbett had planned for her and the other women at the Roxette, I was livid. And I was determined to do whatever I could to stop it happening. My mam and da have endured too bloody much already; they deserve not to have the rug pulled out from under them one more time.

After we'd had our tea, Da and I went down to the club. But I only stayed long enough to do some basic research. I had other fish to fry. I got on the mobile and arranged to meet up with Liz's daughters, Lauren and Shayla. Like me, they found a way out of the poverty trap that has our town between its teeth. They were always into computers, even at school. They both went to college and got qualifications in IT and now they run their own computer consultancy up in

Newcastle. I had the germ of an idea, and I knew they'd help me make it a reality.

We met up in a nice little country pub over by Bishop Auckland. I told them what Corbett had in mind, and they were as angry as me. And when I laid out the bare bones of my plan, they were on board before I was half a dozen sentences into it. Right from the off, they were on side, coming up with their own ideas for making it even stronger and more foolproof.

It was Shayla who came up with the idea of getting Corbett to suck me off. At first, I was revolted. I thought it was grotesque. Over the top. Too cruel. I'll be honest. I've swung both ways in my time. Working in theatre and telly, there's plenty of opportunities to explore the wilder shores of experience. But having a bit of fun with somebody you fancy is a far cry from letting some sleaze like Corbett anywhere near your tackle.

'I'd never be able to get it up,' I protested.

They both laughed. 'You're a bloke,' Lauren said dismissively. 'And you're an actor. Just imagine he's Jennifer Aniston.'

'Or Brad Pitt,' Shayla giggled.

'I think even Olivier might have had problems with that,' I sighed, knowing I was outgunned and outnumbered. It was clear to me that now I'd brought them aboard, the two women were going to figure out a battle plan in which I was to be the foot soldier, the cannon fodder and the SAS, all rolled into one.

The first – and the most difficult – thing we had to do was to plant a fibre-optic camera in Corbett's lounge. We tossed around various ideas, all of which were both complicated and risky. Finally, Lauren hit on the answer. 'His lad's about twelve, thirteen, isn't he?' she asked.

I nodded. 'So I heard down the club.'

'That's sorted then,' she said. 'I can get hold of some games that are at the beta-testing stage. We can knock up a letter telling Darren he's been chosen to test the games. Offer him a fee. Then I pick my moment, roll up at the house before he gets home. She's bound to invite me in and make me a cup of tea. I'll find somewhere to plant the camera and we're rolling.'

And that's exactly how it played out. Lauren got into the house, and while Margo Corbett was off making her a brew, she stuck the camera in the middle of a dried flower arrangement. Perfect.

The next phase was the most frustrating. We had to wait till we had the right set of pictures to make the scam work. For three nights, we filmed Corbett's living-room, biting our nails, wondering how long it would take for mother and son to sit down together and watch something with enough dramatic tension. We cracked it on the Monday night, when Channel Five was showing a horror movie. Darren and Margo sat next to each other, huddling closer as the climaxes piled up.

Then it was Shayla's turn. She spent the rest of Monday night and most of Tuesday putting together the short digital film that we would use to make sure Corbett did what he was told. Lauren had already filmed me against a blue background waving around the replica sawn-off shotgun we'd used as a prop last series. It hadn't been hard to liberate it from the props store. They're incredibly sloppy, those guys. Shayla cut the images in so it looked like I was standing in the Corbett's living-room threatening his nearest and dearest. I have to say, the end result was impressive and, more importantly, convincing.

Now we were ready. We chose Wednesday night to strike. Lauren had managed to get hold of her mam's keys and copied the one for the Roxette's back door. While the last session of the evening was in full swing, she'd slipped out and unlocked the door so I could walk straight in.

It all went better than I feared. You'd have thought Corbett was working from the same script, the way he caved in and did what he was told. And in spite of my fears, the girls had been right. My body didn't betray us.

I made my getaway without a problem and drove straight to Newcastle. Shayla got to work on the video, transferring it to digital, doing the edit and transferring it back to VHS tape again. I packed the money into a box and addressed it to Children in Need, ready to go in the post in the morning, then settled down to wait for Shayla.

The finished video was a masterpiece. We'd all been in Tyson Herbert's office for a drink at one time or another, so we knew where the video camera was. I'd been careful to keep my body between the camera and the gun for as much time as possible, which meant Shayla had been able to incorporate quite a lot of the original video. We had footage of Corbett packing the money into the holdall. Even better, we had the full blow job on tape without a single frame that showed the gun.

The final challenge was to deliver the video to Corbett without either the police or his wife knowing about it. In the end, we went for something we'd done on a stupid TV spy series I'd had a small part in a couple of years previously. We waited till he'd set off in the car, heading down the A1 towards our town. I followed him at a discreet distance then I called him on his mobile.

'Hello, Keith. This is your friend from last night.'

'You fucking cunt.'

'That's no way to speak to a man whose dick you've had in your mouth,' I said, going as menacing as I could manage. 'Listen to me. Three point four miles past the next exit, there's a lay-by. Pull over and take a look in the rubbish bin. You'll find something there that might interest you.' I cut the call and dialled Lauren. 'He's on his way,' I told her.

'OK, I'll make the drop.'

I came off the dual carriageway at the exit before the lay-by. I waited three minutes, then got back on the road. When I passed the lay-by, Corbett was standing by the bin, the padded envelope in his hand.

I sped past, then called him again a few minutes later. 'These are the edited highlights,' I told him. 'I'll call you in an hour when you've had a chance to check it out.'

He wasn't any happier when I made the call. 'You bastard,' he exploded. 'You total fucking bastard. You've made it look like we were in it together.'

'So we are, Keith,' I said calmly. 'You do something for me, and I won't send copies of the tape to the cops and your wife.'

'You blackmailing piece of shit,' he shouted.

'I'll take that as a yes, shall I?'

* * *

NOREEN

You could have knocked me down with a feather. I didn't know what to expect when I turned up that Thursday for work, but it wasn't what happened. I knew about the robbery by then – the whole town was agog. I thought the Cobra would be pretty shaken up, but I didn't expect a complete personality change.

Before I'd even got my coat off, he was in the staff-room, all smiles and gritted teeth. 'Noreen,' he said. 'A word, please?'

'How are you feeling, Mr Corbett?' I asked. 'That must have been a terrible experience.'

He looked away, almost as if he was ashamed. 'I don't want to discuss it.' He cleared his throat. 'Noreen, I might have been a bit hasty the other day. I've come to realise how much of the atmosphere at the Roxette depends on you and the girls.'

I couldn't believe my ears. I couldn't think of a single word to say. I just stood there with my mouth open.

'So, if you'd be willing to stay on, I'd like to offer you your job back.'

'What about the other girls? Liz and Jackie and Julie?' I couldn't have accepted if they weren't in the deal.

He nodded, although it looked as if the movement gave him pain. 'All four of you. Full reinstatement.'

'That's very generous of you,' I managed to say. Though what I really wanted was to ask him if he'd taken a blow to the head during the robbery.

He grimaced, his tight little face closed as a pithead. 'And if you still want to do the Children in Need night, we could make it next Friday,' he added, each word sounding like it was choked out of him.

'Thank you,' I said. I took a quick look out of the window to see if there were any pigs flying past, but no. Whatever had happened inside the Cobra's head, the rest of the world seemed to be going on as normal.

And he was as good as his word. I don't know what changed his mind, but the four calling birds are back behind the balls at the Roxette. I still can't quite believe it, but as our Dickson reminded me, I've always said there's good in everybody. Sometimes, you just have to dig deep to find it.

The Consolation Blonde

Awards are meaningless, right? They're always political, they're forgotten two days later and they always go to the wrong book, right? Well, that's what we all say when the prize goes somewhere else. Of course, it's a different story when it's our turn to stand at the podium and thank our agents, our partners and our pets. Then, naturally enough, it's an honor and a thrill.

That's what I was hoping I'd be doing that October night in New York. I had been nominated for Best Novel in the Speculative Fiction category of the US Book Awards, the national literary prizes that carry not only prestige but also a fifty thousand dollar check for the winners. *Termagant Fire*, the concluding novel in my *King's Infidel* trilogy, had broken all records for a fantasy novel. More weeks in the *New York Times* bestseller list than King, Grisham and Cornwell put together. And the reviews had been breathtaking, referring to *Termagant Fire* as 'the first novel since Tolkien to make fantasy respectable'. Fans and booksellers alike had voted it their book of the year. Serious literary critics had examined the parallels between my fantasy universe and America in the defining epoch of the Sixties. Now all I was waiting for was the imprimatur of the judges in the nation's foremost literary prize.

Not that I was taking it for granted. I know how fickle judges can be, how much they hate being told what to think by the rest of the world. I understood only too well that the *succes d'estime* the book had enjoyed could be the very factor that would snatch my moment of glory from my grasp. I had already given myself a stiff talking-to in my hotel bathroom mirror, reminding myself of the dangers of hubris. I needed to keep my feet on the ground, and maybe failing to win the golden prize would be the best thing that could happen to me. At least it would be one less thing to have to live up to with the next book.

But on the night, I took it as a good sign that my publisher's table at the awards dinner was right down at the front of the room, smack bang up against the podium. They never like the winners being seated too far from the stage just in case the applause doesn't last long enough for them to make it up there ahead of the silence.

My award was third from last in the litany of winners. That meant a long time sitting still and looking interested. But I could only cling onto the fragile conviction that it was all going to be worth it in the end. Eventually, the knowing Virginia drawl of the MC, a middle-ranking news anchorman, got us there. I arranged my face in a suitably bland expression, which I was glad of seconds later when the name he announced was not mine. There followed a short, stunned silence, then, with more eyes on me than on her, the victor weaved her way to the front of the room to a shadow of the applause previous winners had garnered.

I have no idea what graceful acceptance speech she came out with. I couldn't tell you who won the remaining two categories. All my energy was channeled into not showing the rage and pain churning inside me. No matter how much I told myself I had prepared for this, the reality was horrible.

At the end of the apparently interminable ceremony, I got to my feet like an automaton. My team formed a sort of flying wedge around me; editor ahead of me, publicist to one side, publisher to the other. 'Let's get you out of here. We don't need pity,' my publisher growled, head down, broad shoulders a challenge to anyone who wanted to offer condolences.

By the time we made it to the bar, we'd acquired a small support crew, ones I had indicated were acceptable by a nod or a word. There was Robert, my first mentor and oldest buddy in the business; Shula, an English sf writer who had become a close friend; Shula's girlfriend Caroline; and Cassie, the manager of the city's premier sf and fantasy bookstore. That's what you need at a time like this, people around who won't ever hold it against you that you vented your spleen in an unseemly way at the moment when your dream turned to ashes. Fuck nobility. I wanted to break something.

But I didn't have the appetite for serious drinking, especially when my vanquisher arrived in the same bar with her celebration in tow. I finished my Jack Daniels and pushed off from the enveloping sofa. 'I'm not much in the mood,' I said. 'I think I'll just head back to my hotel.'

'You're at the InterCon, right?' Cassie asked.

'Yeah.'

'I'll walk with you, I'm going that way.'

'Don't you want to join the winning team?' I asked, jerking my head towards the barks of laughter by the bar.

Cassie put her hand on my arm. 'You wrote the best book, John. That's victory enough for me.'

I made my excuses and we walked into a ridiculously balmy New York evening. I wanted snow and ice to match my mood, and said as much to Cassie.

Her laugh was low. 'The pathetic fallacy,' she said. 'You writers just never got over that, did you? Well, John, if you're going to cling to that notion, you better change your mood to match the weather.'

I snorted. 'Easier said than done.'

'Not really,' said Cassie. 'Look, we're almost at the Inter-Con. Let's have a drink.'

'OK.'

'On one condition. We don't talk about the award, we don't talk about the asshole who won it, we don't talk about how wonderful your book is and how it should have been recognised tonight.'

I grinned. 'Cassie, I'm a writer. If I can't talk about me, what the hell else does that leave?'

She shrugged and steered me into the lobby. 'Gardening? Gourmet food? Favorite sexual positions? Music?'

We settled in a corner of the bar, me with Jack on the rocks, she with a Cosmopolitan. We ended up talking about movies, past and present, finding to our surprise that in spite of our affiliation to the sf and fantasy world, what we both actually loved most was *film noir*. Listening to Cassie talk, watching her push her blonde hair back from her eyes, enjoying the sly smiles that crept out when she said something witty or sardonic, I forgot the slings and arrows and enjoyed myself.

When they announced last call at midnight, I didn't want it to end. It seemed natural enough to invite her up to my room to continue the conversation. Sure, at the back of my mind was the possibility that it might end with those long legs wrapped around mine, but that really wasn't the most important thing. What mattered was that Cassie had taken my mind off what ailed me. She had already provided consolation enough, and I wanted it to go on. I didn't want to be left alone with my rancor and self-pity or any of the other uglinesses that were fighting for space inside me.

She sprawled on the bed. It was that or an armchair, which offered little prospect of comfort. I mixed drinks, finding it hard not to imagine sliding those tight black trousers over her hips or running my hands under that black silk tee, or pushing the long shimmering overblouse off her shoulders so I could cover them with kisses.

I took the drinks over and she sat up, crossing her legs in a full lotus and straightening her spine. 'I thought you were really dignified tonight,' she said.

'Didn't we have a deal? That tonight was off limits?' I lay on my side, carefully not touching her at any point.

'That was in the bar. You did well, sticking to it. Think you earned a reward?'

'What kind of reward?'

'I give a mean backrub,' she said, looking at me over the rims of her glasses. 'And you look tense.'

'A backrub would be . . . very acceptable,' I said.

Cassie unfolded her legs and stood up. 'OK. I'll go into the bathroom and give you some privacy to get undressed. Oh, and John – strip right down to the skin. I can't do your lower back properly if I have to fuck about with waistbands and stuff.'

I couldn't quite believe how fast things were moving. We hadn't been in the room ten minutes, and here was Cassie instructing me to strip for her. OK, it wasn't quite like that sounds, but it was equally a perfectly legitimate description of events. The sort of thing you could say to the guys and they would make a set of assumptions from. If, of course, you were the sort of sad asshole who felt the need to validate himself like that.

I took my clothes off, draping them over the armchair without actually folding them, then lay face down on the bed. I wished I'd spent more of the spring working out than I had writing. But I knew my shoulders were still respectable, my legs strong and hard, even if I was carrying a few more pounds around the waist than I would have liked.

I heard the bathroom door open and Cassie say, 'You ready, John?'

I was very, very ready. Somehow, it wasn't entirely a surprise that it wasn't just the skin of her hands that I felt against mine.

How did I know it had to be her? I dreamed her hands. Nothing slushy or sentimental; just her honest hands with their strong square fingers, the palms slightly callused from the daily shunting of books from carton to shelf, the play of muscle and skin over blood and bone. I dreamed her hands and woke with tears on my face. That was the day I called Cassie and said I had to see her again.

'I don't think so.' Her voice was cautious, and not, I believed, simply because she was standing behind the counter in the bookstore.

'Why not? I thought you enjoyed it,' I said. 'Did you think it was just a one-night stand?'

'Why would I imagine it could be more? You're a married man, you live in Denver, you're good looking and successful. Why on earth would I set myself up for a let-down by expecting a repeat performance? John, I am so not in the business of being the Other Woman. A one-night stand is just fine, but I don't do affairs.'

'I'm not married.' It was the first thing I could think of to say. That it was the truth was simply a bonus.

'What do you mean, you're not married? It says so on your book jackets. You mention her in interviews.' Now there was an edge of anger, a 'don't fuck with me' note in her voice.

'I've never been married. I lied about it.'

A long pause. 'Why would you lie about being married?' she demanded.

'Cassie, you're in the store, right? Look around you. Scope out the women in there. Now, I hate to hurt people's feelings. Do you see why I might lie about my marital status?'

I could hear the gurgle of laughter swelling and bursting down the telephone line. 'John, you are a bastard, you know that? A charming bastard, but a bastard nevertheless. You mean that? About never having been married?'

'There is no moral impediment to you and me fucking each other's brains out as often as we choose to. Unless, of course, there's someone lurking at home waiting for you?' I tried to keep my voice light. I'd been torturing myself with that idea every since our night together. She'd woken me with soft kisses just after five, saying she had to go. By the time we'd said our farewells, it had been nearer six and she'd finally scrambled away from me, saying she had to get home and change before she went into open the store. It had made sense, but so too did the possibility of her sneaking back into the cold side of a double bed somewhere down in Chelsea or SoHo.

Now, she calmed my twittering heart. 'There's nobody. Hasn't been for over a year now. I'm free as you, by the sounds of it.'

'I can be in New York at the weekend,' I said. 'Can I stay?'

'Sure,' Cassie said, her voice somehow promising much more than a simple word.

That was the start of something unique in my experience. With Cassie, I found a sense of completeness I'd never known before. I'd always scoffed at terms like 'soul mate', but Cassie forced me to eat the words baked in a humble pie. We matched. It was as simple as that. She compensated for my lacks, she allowed me space to demonstrate my strengths. She made me feel like the finest lover who had ever laid hands on her. She was also the first woman I'd ever had a relationship with who miraculously never complained that the writing got in the way. With Cassie, everything was possible and life seemed remarkably straightforward.

She gave me all the space I needed, never minding that my fantasy world sometimes seemed more real to me than what was for dinner. And I did the same for her, I thought. I didn't dog her steps at the store, turning up for every event like an autograph hunter. I only came along to see writers I would have gone to see anyway; old friends, new kids on the block who were doing interesting work, visiting foreign names. I encouraged her to keep up her girls' nights out, barely registering when she rolled home in the small hours smelling of smoke and tasting of Triple Sec.

She didn't mind that I refused to attempt her other love, rock climbing; forty-year-old knees can't learn that sort of new trick. But equally, I never expected her to give it up for me, and even though she usually scheduled her overnight climbing trips for when I was out of town on book business, that was her choice rather than my demand. Bless her, she never tried taking advantage of our relationship to nail down better discount deals with my publishers, and I respected her even more for that.

Commuting between Denver and New York lasted all of two months. Then in the same week, I sold my house and my agent sold the *King's Infidel* trilogy to Oliver Stone's company for enough money for me actually to be able to buy a Manhattan apartment that was big enough for both of us and our several thousand books. I loved, and felt loved in return. It was as if I was leading a charmed life.

I should have known better. I am, after all, an adherent of the genre of fiction where pride always, always, always comes before a very nasty fall.

We'd been living together in the kind of bliss that makes one's friends gag and one's enemies weep for almost a year when the accident happened. I know that Freudians claim there is never any such thing as accident, but it's hard to see how anyone's subconscious could have felt the world would end up a better or more moral place because of this particular mishap.

My agent was in the middle of a very tricky negotiation with my publisher over my next deal. They were horse-trading and haggling hard over the money on the table, and my agent was naturally copying me in on the e-mails. One morning, I logged on to find that day's update had a file attachment with it. 'Hi, John,' the e-mail read.

You might be interested to see that they're getting so nitty-gritty about this deal that they're actually discussing your

last year's touring and miscellaneous expenses. Of course,
I wasn't supposed to see this attachment, but we all know
what an idiot Tom is when it comes to electronics. Great
editor; cyber-idiot. Anyway, I thought you might find it
amusing to see how much they reckon they spent on you.
See how it tallies with your recollections ...

I wasn't much drawn to the idea, but since the attachment
was there, I thought I might as well take a look. It never
hurts to get a little righteous indignation going about how
much hotels end up billing for a one-night stay. It's the sup-
plementaries that are the killers. Fifteen dollars for a bottle of
water was the best I came across on last year's tour. Needless
to say, I stuck a glass under the tap. Even when it's someone
else's dime, I hate to encourage the robber barons who mas-
querade as hoteliers.

I was drifting down through the list when I ran into something out of the basic rhythm of hotels, taxis, airfares, author
escorts. 'Consolation Blonde, $500', I read.

I knew what the words meant, but I didn't understand
their linkage. Especially not on my expense list. If I'd spent
it, you'd think I'd know what it was.

Then I saw the date.

My stomach did a back flip. Some dates you never forget.
Like the US Book Awards dinner.

I didn't want to believe it, but I had to be certain. I called
Shula's girlfriend Caroline, herself an editor of mystery
fiction in one of the big London houses. Once we'd got the
small talk out of the way, I cut to the chase. 'Caroline, have
you ever heard the term "consolation blonde" in publishing
circles?'

'Where did you hear that, John?' she asked, answering the question inadvertently.

'I overheard it in one of those chi-chi midtown bars where literary publishers hang out. I was waiting to meet my agent, and I heard one guy say to the other, "He was OK after the consolation blonde." I wasn't sure what it meant but I thought it sounded like a great title for a short story.'

Caroline gave that well-bred middle-class Englishwoman's giggle. 'I suppose you could be right. What can I say here, John? This really is one of publishing's tackier areas. Basically, it's what you lay on for an author who's having a bad time. Maybe they didn't win an award they thought was in the bag, maybe their book has bombed, maybe they're having a really bad tour. So you lay on a girl, a nice girl. A fan, a groupie, a publicity girlie, bookseller, whatever. Somebody on the fringes, not a hooker as such. Tell them how nice it would be for poor old what's-his-name to have a good time. So the sad boy gets the consolation blonde and the consolation blonde gets a nice boost to her bank account plus the bonus of being able to boast about shagging a name. Even if it's a name that nobody else in the pub has ever heard before.'

I felt I'd lost the power of speech. I mumbled something and managed to end the call without screaming my anguish at Caroline. In the background, I could hear Bob Dylan singing 'Idiot Wind'. Cassie had set the CD playing on repeat before she'd left for work and now the words mocked me for the idiot I was.

Cassie was my consolation blonde.

I wondered how many other disappointed men had been lifted up by the power of her fingers and made to feel strong again? I wondered whether she'd have stuck around for more than that one-night stand if I'd been a poor man. I wondered how many times she'd slid into bed with me after a night out, not with the girls, but wearing the mantle of the consolation blonde. I wondered whether pity was still the primary emotion that moved her when she moaned and arched her spine for me.

I wanted to break something. And this time, I wasn't going to be diverted.

I've made a lot of money for my publisher over the years. So when I show up to see my editor, Tom, without an appointment, he makes space and time for me.

That day, I could tell inside a minute that he wished for once he'd made an exception. He looked like he wasn't sure whether he should just cut out the middle-man and throw himself out of the twenty-third-floor window. 'I don't know what you're talking about,' he yelped in response to my single phrase.

'Bullshit,' I yelled. 'You hired Cassie to be my consolation blonde. There's no point in denying it, I've seen the paperwork.'

'You're mistaken, John,' Tom said desperately, his alarmed chipmunk eyes widening in dilemma.

'No. Cassie was my consolation blonde for the US Book Awards. You didn't know I was going to lose, so you must have set her up in advance, as a stand-by. Which means you must have used her before.'

'I swear, John, I swear to God, I don't know . . .' Whatever Tom was going to say got cut off by me grabbing his stupid preppie tie and yanking him out of his chair.

'Tell me the truth,' I growled, dragging him towards the

window. 'It's not like it can be worse than I've imagined. How many of my friends has she fucked? How many five-hundred-buck one-night stands have you pimped for my girlfriend since we got together? How many times have you and your buddies laughed behind my back because the woman I love is playing consolation blonde to somebody else? Tell me, Tom. Tell me the truth before I throw you out of this fucking window. Because I don't have any more to lose.'

'It's not like that,' he gibbered. I smelled piss and felt a warm dampness against my knee. His humiliation was sweet, though it was a poor second to what he'd done to me.

'Stop lying,' I screamed. He flinched as my spittle spattered his face. I shook him like a terrier with a rat.

'OK, OK,' he sobbed. 'Yes, Cassie was a consolation blonde. Yes, I hired her last year for you at the awards banquet. But I swear, that was the last time. She wrote me a letter, said after she met you she couldn't do this again. John, the letter's in my files. She never cashed the check for being with you. You have to believe me. She fell in love with you that first night and she never did it again.'

The worst of it was, I could tell he wasn't lying. But still, I hauled him over to the filing cabinets and made him produce his evidence. The letter was everything he'd promised. It was dated the day after our first encounter, two whole days before I called her to ask if I could see her again.

Dear Tom,
I'm returning your $500 cheque. It's not appropriate for me to accept it this time. I won't be available to do close author escort work in future. Meeting John

Treadgold has changed things for me. I can't thank you enough for introducing us.
Good luck.
Cassie White

I stood there, reading her words, every one cutting me like the wounds I'd carved into her body the night before.

I guess they don't have awards ceremonies in prison. Which is probably just as well, given what a bad loser I turned out to be.

Metamorphosis

Fingers rippling down my spine. Lips nuzzling my neck. Trimmed fingernails leaving their marks on my skin like vapour trails in a clear blue sky. Teeth nibbling my shoulder blades, sinking into the long muscles of my back. Hands fierce on my buttocks, clawing and spreading them. A tongue rimming me, unimagined waves of pleasure spreading deep inside me from the tight scrunch of my anus. A fist forcing its way into me, so deep I think I'm going to split open. Like when I gave birth. The smell of sex and sweat and something more earthy. The sound of a voice I barely recognise as mine, moaning, 'I'm your bitch, fuck me harder.' The moans that turn to cries as my body gives itself up to her.

How the hell did I get here?

I'm a stranger in my own skin. Nobody who knows me would recognise this wanton sprawled on a hotel-room bed, possessed by a desire I never even thought to conjure before. I never fantasised about having sex with a woman. I never fantasised about dirty, nasty sex. I've always been a soft-focus sort of girl. Candles meant romantic flicker to me, not hot wax on nipples.

Yet now this strange addiction has me in its grip.

I tell myself the story of how it came to this, and I am none the wiser. I list the chain of circumstances, as I am trained to do, and it still sounds entirely alien, something so far outside my life that it can have no connection to me.

Cause and effect, action and reaction, the steady building of a case. That's what I do for a living, and that is where the story begins. I am Jane Sullivan, barrister at law, called at Middle Temple twelve years ago. I am a criminal barrister on the Northern Circuit. I am a happily married woman with two daughters aged nine and seven. My husband David is a lecturer in philosophy at Manchester University. We live in a three-storey Victorian house in a quiet cul-de-sac in the part of Didsbury that hasn't been colonised by students and young graduates taking the first steps in their careers. We have two Volvos and a Labrador called Sam.

We are embarrassingly middle-class. And I like my life.

So how the hell did I get here, groaning with animal delight at the hands of a woman with six body piercings and three tattoos?

Stevie walked into my life and my chambers six months ago. The client was accused of attempted murder, the solicitor not one of my usual providers of briefs. They'd come over from Leeds on the recommendation of a local client who thought I'd done a good job in a similar case earlier in the year. Stevie was there at the con to give the client moral support. The story was broadly familiar, though not one I hear nearly often enough.

The client had been living in a women's refuge after her boyfriend had put her into hospital once too often. In spite of a restraining order, the boyfriend had tracked her down and burst into the refuge. He'd found her in the kitchen, and in his haste to attack her, he'd slipped and fallen. Simultaneously, she'd had the presence of mind to smash the milk bottle she'd been holding against the edge of the sink. As he stumbled to his feet, she'd stabbed him in the neck with the jagged edge. And now she was the one facing the full weight of the law. Stevie, it turned out, worked part-time at the refuge while completing her masters degree in psychology. The client trusted her, which wasn't something she could say about many people she'd met in her twenty-three years.

To be honest, I didn't pay much attention to Stevie that day. I registered the black hair, the dark brows, the blue eyes and the creamy pale skin that signals a particular set of Irish genes, but I felt not a flicker of attraction. My focus was on the client, my mind already racing through the possibilities of having the charge reduced to a Section Eighteen wounding.

I took instructions, gave as much reassurance as I could, then went home to read my children a bedtime story and eat supper with my husband. I didn't give Stevie another thought until the case was called at Leeds Crown Court.

The client was shivering with fear and Stevie was rubbing her hands when we met outside the robing room. The client was beyond sensible discussion, so I directed my points at Stevie. I explained that I'd already seen the prosecution counsel and he wasn't inclined to reduce the charges. However, I thought that might paradoxically work in our favour; a jury would be more reluctant to convict on the greater charge once they had heard the evidence of what the victim had done to my client in the past. I was intent on running the self-defence line. Anyone who had suffered what my client had suffered at this man's hands would have reasonable grounds to be in fear of her life.

The trial didn't go well. My client was the worst kind of witness; defensive, contradictory, inarticulate. The victim cleaned up well and managed a good stab at the heartbroken remorseful lover role. But I was determined not to lose this one, and even if I say so myself, I delivered the kind of closing address to the jury that barristers have wet dreams about. The judge summed up late on the second day, and I fully expected the jury to be out overnight. That's why I'd kept on my hotel room.

But to my delight, they came back inside half an hour, and with a not-guilty verdict. I congratulated the client, who was a soggy bundle of tears by then, shook hands with Stevie and headed back for my hotel to pack my bags and catch a train back to Manchester.

I'd barely thrown off my suit jacket when there was a knock on the door. I opened it, expecting housekeeping, or the man who recharges the minibar. Instead, Stevie was lounging casually against the doorjamb, a bottle of champagne dangling from her hand. 'I thought you might fancy a little celebration,' she said.

'I was just about to check out.'

One corner of Stevie's mouth lifted in a half-smile, a dimple creasing her cheek. 'Go on, you know you want to,' she said. 'That was a helluva performance in there. You deserve the chance to rerun it with somebody who knows you're not bullshitting.'

'I really should . . .'

'Besides, nobody's expecting you back in Manchester, are they? We all thought this was going to run into tomorrow.' She raised the bottle and waggled it gently. It was, I couldn't help noticing, rather a good marque.

In spite of myself, I was smiling back at her. I opened the door. 'Why not?' I said. If I'd known the answer to that question, I'd have slammed the door in her face.

I got a couple of glasses out of the minibar and we sat in

the armchairs on either side of the little round table in the window. The last of the light glinted on the tiny fragments of diamond that crusted the outer rim of her eyebrow ring. Stevie opened the bottle with remarkably little fuss and poured the champagne into the tilted glasses. 'Here's to crime,' she said. We clinked and sipped. 'You were fantastic in there, you know. I thought we were goners, but you turned the whole thing round.'

I shrugged. 'It's what they pay me for.'

She shook her head. 'It was a lot more than that. I've seen enough barristers in action to know the difference. You were very special today.'

I felt mildly flustered; I could sense an edge of flirtation in her voice and I wasn't sure whether I was imagining it. 'I'm supposed always to be special,' I blurted out.

She gave her crooked smile again. 'I don't doubt you manage it.' She nudged the ashtray on the table with a long, slim finger. 'Do you mind if I smoke?'

'Feel free. It's not as if I'm going to be spending the night here.'

She opened her shoulder bag and took out a tobacco tin. To my astonishment, she started rolling a joint. 'You've been walking around in the court with a pocketful of dope?' I knew I probably sounded like her mother, but I couldn't help myself.

Stevie grinned. 'Hardly a pocketful. About a caution's worth, I'd say. Jane, nobody was interested in me today. I could have been shooting up smack in the ladies' loo and they'd never have noticed.' She must have caught my look of horror, because she added hastily, 'Not that I touch the hard stuff. Only joking.'

She lit the joint and took a deep drag on it, holding the smoke for a good fifteen seconds, her eyes closed in pleasure. Then she held it out to me, her eyebrows raised in an amused question.

I don't know why I took it. Perhaps I wanted to show her I wasn't as straight as she assumed. Perhaps I wanted to revisit the carefree student I'd once been, before ambition and its satisfaction had given me too much to be willing to lose. Or perhaps I had the first subconscious inkling that there might be something lurking beneath the surface here that I'd require an excuse for afterwards.

Whatever the reason, I shared that joint. And the next one. The champagne slipped down, and we began to unwind, our public faces unravelling as we shared something of our stories. It seemed to make sense to order another bottle of champagne from room service. We were halfway through the second bottle when Stevie said, 'I should be going. If you're heading back to Manchester, you'll need to think about getting a train.'

My dismay startled me. I didn't want her to go, and that shook me. But I couldn't remember the last time I'd felt so relaxed. She got to her feet and moved towards the door. I couldn't think of a way to stop her, so I followed. She opened the door and turned towards me. 'I'll say goodnight, then.' She stepped forward and kissed me.

My mouth was open under hers. I felt the flicker of her tongue inside my lower lip. Then my hand was in her hair, pulling her into me, the blood pounding in my ears. Suddenly we separated. I couldn't read her eyes. I had no idea if she could see the darkness of the desire in mine.

'I don't think it's a very good idea to stand snogging in a

hotel doorway,' she said coolly. 'Don't you think you'd better close the door?'

A wave of mortification brought a red flush to my neck. 'I'm sorry,' I said, every inch the stiff lady barrister again. I stepped back to shut the door, but before I could, she was inside the room.

'You do want me on this side of it, don't you?' It was, we both knew, an entirely rhetorical question.

A tangle of clothes and limbs, a stumble of legs and hands, a mumble of words and lips, and we were naked on the bed. There was nothing seductive or sensual in it; we'd performed the foreplay with our earlier words. This was simply a total carnality I'd never known before. It was appetite fed, satisfied, then fresh hunger aroused purely to be appeased. Time slid past us in a chaos of glutted lust. She did things to me I had never known I desired. And without giving it a second thought, I acquiesced.

More than that, I gave as good as I got. I discovered instincts I didn't know I possessed. My mouth, my hands performed with a sureness of touch I couldn't have believed possible. Language was reduced to a primal state. 'There . . . oh yes. Harder . . . Please . . . Oh God . . .'

Somewhere around dawn, I think, we slept. I woke to find her sprawled face down next to me, the tail end of a sheet across the hollow of her back. The room reeked of sex, with a sweet base note of marijuana. The clock read 7:34, and I remembered my life. David would be getting the girls up, ready for the school run. He'd wonder why I hadn't called the night before, but not in an anxious way. He knew that when I was absorbed in a case, I didn't always want to be dragged into a different, distracting mental space.

I knew I should be consumed with guilt, but it was entirely absent. All I felt was a kind of grateful wonder, an astonishment that there was room in my life for something so remarkable.

Stevie stirred and lifted her head. Her eyes opened a crack and she laughed softly. 'I thought you'd be long gone, beating yourself up all the way to Manchester,' she drawled.

'I want to see you again.' The words tumbled out before I could consider their wisdom.

'I know you do. And you will.' She propped herself up and kissed me. 'Like the song says, we've only just begun.'

I travelled back on the train, understanding for the first time the notion of the body electric. I was tingling in every limb, invigorated and exhilarated. I'd thought I understood the power of sex, but I'd been seeing a coloured world in monochrome.

Of course, I had already convinced myself that this was an entirely physical thing. It belonged in the domain of the senses, not in the heart. As such, there would be no real and present danger in seeing Stevie again. We would be occasional lovers, it would gradually lose its glamour and we would drift apart. My only real concern was whether Stevie would fall in love with me. If that were to happen, it might pose a threat to my life. But somehow, I didn't think that was probable. I couldn't see Stevie picturing a future with someone as conventional as me.

What never occurred to me was that I would be the one who would become besotted. I saw her again the week after the Leeds trial, down in London. This time, the sex was more extreme, more rooted in the exploration of outrageous fantasy. This time, there was cocaine to sharpen the edge of desire and loosen my non-existent inhibitions. It enraptured me. I was hooked on her.

I found myself seeking out briefs that would take me away from home so I could spend the nights with Stevie. I couldn't get through the day without talking to her on the phone, conversations that always revolved around sex and usually ended in orgasm. I knew my advocacy was suffering, because I was spending more time mooning after Stevie than I was absorbing my briefs. I was taking the kind of risks that could have destroyed my life and the lives of the people I had, until Stevie, loved more than anything in the world.

That, then, is the chain of circumstance that has brought me here, brought me to my knees again before a woman who is clearly tiring of me. She makes excuses now where before she made plans. Sometimes, when I call, there is someone else there and she won't talk. And I cannot bear the thought of her lying in someone else's arms, this woman who has stolen my comfort and ripped a hole in the fabric of my life. A day without the sound of her voice leaves me hollow, picking at my food, snapping at my children.

I fear what I will do when she leaves me. I know now what it is to be driven by an obsession that is beyond control. I understand the mentality of stalkers, because that is what I am becoming. Her leaving me will bring my house down in ruins about me because I will not be able to let her walk away. The need in me is too fierce.

I fear what I am becoming. I look in the mirror in the morning and see an edge of madness in my own gaze. I have run too many defences not to know the damage that this could wreak if I let it spiral further out of control. The only thing I can do to save myself, to save my life, is to act now, while I am still capable of organised, rational thought. If I wait till she leaves me, as she undoubtedly will, I shall be beyond such niceties.

And so I have made my plans. This will be our last night together. The room is booked in Stevie's name. What she doesn't know is that I have already ostentatiously checked into another room in a motel on the far side of town; the sort of place where nobody sees you come or go. I made sure she got here first tonight, and I will sit it out until I can lose myself in the early morning departures and go straight to court. I've been very careful not to touch anything that would take a fingerprint; I know better than to wipe down the surfaces, because that would be a sure sign that someone else had been here with her.

We're going to play bondage games tonight. I asked her to bring her toys with her, and she has, because she still cares enough to want to give me pleasure. I've been reading up on cases of autoerotic asphyxiation. It's mostly a male thing, but there have been cases where women have died playing the sort of games that are supposed to enhance sexual pleasure. I've worked it all out. Her feet bound to the foot of the iron bedstead. Her hands tied in front of her. The orange spiked with poppers in her mouth. Then the noose round her neck, fastened to the bed head.

The tragic accident.

The hardest part will be avoiding her eyes.

When Larry Met Allie

We'd done virtually everything before we even met.

Let me rephrase that. We'd done, virtually, everything before we even met. Or perhaps, we'd done virtually everything, virtually, before we met. Amazing what a difference a couple of commas can make.

The difference between life and death, sometimes.

I chose her very carefully. I knew what I was looking for. Distance was a key factor; I didn't want there to be any possibility of her appearing in my world. No witnesses, you see. That she already had a lover was also important; there had to be a good reason for her to keep me clandestine. I didn't want her beautiful, either; beautiful women are accustomed to having men come on to them. They know how to brush us off and they don't think twice about it. As every teenage boy knows, the ugly girls are always grateful for attention.

The other vital element in the selection process came from her work. I was looking for a writer who revelled in sensuality, whose work displayed a hunger for the wilder shores of sexual experiment, whose prose had the power to inflame a flicker of desire. There's no shortage of sex in crime fiction these days, but most of it is about as erotic as the *Encyclopaedia Britannica*. I had to plough through a lot of depressingly grim attempts at arousing the reader before I found her.

Allie James. Author of four psychological thrillers featuring FBI profiler Susan Sondheim. None of them had been

New York Times bestsellers, but she had respectable sales and a growing fan base, if her sales ranking and reviews on Amazon.com were to be trusted. I read the books and felt a prickle of excitement run up the back of my neck. On the face of it, she was a prime candidate.

Her protagonist had two lovers during the course of the four novels. Allie's descriptions of their encounters managed to walk the tightrope between graphic mechanics and senti-mental euphemism. There was a genuine erotic charge in what she wrote, a sly, knowing sensuousness that tightened my stomach, dried my mouth and made me want more.

The brief author biog on the back flap was encouraging too. 'Allie James was born and raised in rural North Carolina. She trained in graphic design and worked for ten years in advertising in Chicago. She now lives in Virginia with her partner.' There was no photograph, which made me think that Allie James didn't have a high opinion of her looks. And with her background, she probably wasn't as sophisticated as a big-city girl. She'd be easier to flatter, to convince and to capture.

I needed more information, however. Next stop, the search engine. Google.com gave me a couple of hundred hits, and I worked my way through reviews, through on-line book-sellers, through newsgroup discussion strands on her work until I eventually found a couple of lengthy interviews that coloured in the picture more fully. Allie was thirty-seven, a Gemini only-child who professed to be fascinated by the extremes of human psychology. Her partner taught English literature in a small college in Virginia. They'd been together for eight years. They had no children, but doted on their Weimeraner bitch. And still no photograph anywhere.

I headed off to a site I'd discovered where it's possible to track down who owns domain names. I typed 'alliejames. com' into their search engine. As I'd expected, I was told that the site was already owned. Any writer with any sense has figured out the importance of owning their domain name, even if they're not doing anything with it yet. If they don't register it themselves, they run the risk of being held to ransom by some nerd who's seen the potential of selling it back to them. Or worse, having their name bought by their publisher, to do with as the parent company wishes.

I chose the option that allowed me to find out the site's owner. Most people don't realise this information is readily available, so they don't bother to hide behind their agent or a box number. Allie was one of those who hadn't. Within seconds, I was staring at her address and the phone number I'd already discovered was unlisted. I printed out the details for future reference, then went on-line to set my bait.

From: Lawrence Ryan, Lr25478@hotmail.com
To: Allie James, ajva@alliejames.com
Re: Your books
Dear Allie,
I wanted to write and tell you how much pleasure your books have given me. Few writers achieve the insight into the human condition that you seem to manage so effort-lessly. I love the depth of characterisation in your work, and the way you convey the passion of the hunter for her goal. Susan Sondheim is one of the best-rounded protagonists in the genre, a woman with a heart and soul as well as a brain. As one who toils in the same part of the garden as you, I know how difficult it is to create something genuinely fresh

in the genre. I just wanted to tell you how much I respect what you do.
Best wishes,
Larry Ryan

I had few doubts that my approach would provoke a response. And I was right. Within twelve hours, I had her reply sitting in my in-box.

Dear Larry,

Wow! What an honor to get fan mail from a fellow writer of your achievement! I've been a huge – albeit silent – fan of your work since The Lazarus Angel *was first published over here. Since when, I've had to break the bank to import the UK editions, because I just don't want to wait for your US publisher to catch up :-)*

I'm so thrilled that you enjoy my adventures with Susan. All fan mail is great, of course, but it means so much more to hear it from someone I admire.

So, where are you up to? When can I expect my next fix?

Yours, in awe,

Allie

Of course, I was straight back on to her. There would be a time to keep her hanging on, but not yet.

Allie,
What a charming reply. You certainly know how to flatter!
I didn't expect you even to have heard of me, never mind to have read my books, given the complete lack of promotion my US publishers throw my way. So it goes . . .

< So, where are you up to? When can I expect my next fix?> I've just finished the proofs for my new book, *Night Sweats*, which means I have a blessed period of about three weeks before I begin the next book. I'm afraid NS won't be out for another five months, so you'll have to possess your soul in patience.

Unless, of course, you'd like me to e-mail it to you? I know there's nothing more tedious than to read a book in type-script, but if you can bear it, I'd be happy to let you see it. You can be the first person to read it cold, knowing nothing at all about it . . .

Best

Larry

It was, of course, an offer she couldn't refuse. I'd known that when I made it. This hadn't been part of my original plan, but the fact that she'd read my work short-circuited the long game I'd initially had in mind. It was a gambit that accelerated the pace enormously, and within days we were deep into exchanges about the craft of writing, the business of publishing, the process of getting a book together, and all the other things that outsiders imagine writers talk about all the time. Although, in fact, we seldom do. But it built bridges between us, principally because I let her do most of the running, then made sure I agreed with almost all she said.

Inevitably, the small details of her life began to slide into the e-mails. I discovered the lover was called Jeffrey, that he was a self-obsessed Aquarius who resented Allie's success. Not that she told me this directly. But it wasn't hard to read between the lines. I avoided criticising Jeffrey, concentrating

rather on making myself seem the considerate and support-
ive type. I let slip that my lover had died a couple of years
before and that I hadn't felt able to open up to anyone since.

From there, it was a short step to gentle flirting. Given
that we were by then exchanging between twenty and fifty
e-mails a day, ranging in length from a few sentences to
twenty-k messages, it didn't take long to escalate into something much more intense. We even swapped our favourite
porn sites. Which, of course, both of us only ever accessed in
the interests of research.

One of us might have been telling the truth, but it certainly wasn't me.

When I had to leave town for a couple of days, I told her
I wouldn't have my laptop with me. She sent seventeen messages, regardless.

Of course, we got to the inevitable point where Allie said
Jeffrey was beginning to wonder if she was having an on-line
affair, she was spending so much time on her computer. :-}

So what constitutes an on-line affair?
I think cyber fucking.
Phew. Well, that's all right, then, we've never been in a
private chatroom together . . .
*I certainly don't feel as if we've crossed a line. I'm very open with
you and I share my feelings, but that's what friends do, right? Do
you feel like a line has been crossed?*
No, I don't feel we've crossed a line. I think we've both
danced kind of close to it, but we use humour to bounce
back from the danger zone.
This is not an easy thing to discuss in e-mail. Face to face
or on the phone, you get the verbal and non-verbal cues

from the other person as to whether they're thinking
<Yes, I want to hear more about what you feel about this>
or <DON'T GO THERE>. In e-mail, if you get into these
complex zones, somebody has to put their toe in the water
first then bite their nails till the other party has the time to
deal with it. So, here goes . . . We are very open with each
other and we go places we would neither of us go with
anyone else. We miss each other when we're not in touch.
We've got a lot in common and we connect on many different levels. We've got mutual respect and we laugh a lot
together. It would be disingenuous to deny there is some
sort of attraction between us. But we're neither of us up
for taking chances with your relationship with the man you
live with. So we've found a way to relate that walks that
tightrope.
I think.
What do you think/feel?
I think/feel the same as you. I'm glad this is cleared up. I really
do enjoy our friendship. It's become very, very important to me.
I can't imagine what life was like before. Or what it would be like
without you and your crazy humor that gets me through the
days. You are the best thing that has happened to me for a very
long time, Larry. And that's not to say anything against Jeffrey.
Though I don't think he'd be comfortable with the way we're so
open about sex.;-) I mean, it's kind of like with porn, isn't it? It's
hard to explain it to someone who doesn't like it. What about
you?
I think I'm in more or less the same place as you on this. I
don't want there to be barriers between us, though. That's
really important to me in terms of my relationship with
you.
Same here.

Consciously or not, it was her way of seeing whether the ante was about to be upped. I nearly danced round the room. Hook, line and sinker. I let a couple of weeks go by, then, when I knew Jeffrey was out of town for a couple of nights at some post-modernist seminar, I started to reel her in. First, I planted a couple of lures in that morning's e-mail. Then I called her number.

'Hello?' She sounded more assertive than I'd expected.

'I bet you can't guess who this is,' I said.

'Larry?' Her voice rose an octave.

'Right first time.' I laughed. 'Amazing.'

'How did you get my number?' She sounded bewildered. 'It's unlisted.'

'What kind of stalker would answer a question like that?' I teased.

Now it was her turn to laugh. 'No, but really, tell me how you tracked me down.'

So I did. I could hear the mixture of delight and unease in her voice. She didn't mind me finding out, but it worried her that other, weirder people might be able to find her so easily. 'I need to change that,' she said.

'You really should. After all, the only person who needs to be able to find you already has.'

The ice was broken. We started talking about things we'd been discussing in our recent posts, and I let the conversation glide round to the fresh bait I'd laid that morning. 'Like I said, I wish I had your ability to write credible sex scenes,' I complained. 'I really need to show the interaction between Guy and Zoe, but the more I work on it, the more wooden it gets.'

She bit. Within seconds, we were talking each other

through what I needed to write. Within minutes, we were practising method writing. 'I can't believe you're making me so horny,' she sighed.

'Oh God. Me too . . .' I let the pause hang for a moment while our breathing crossed thousands of miles. 'It would be very bad manners of me to leave you in that state,' I said, aiming for that ironic English politeness that Americans love so much. And of course, she didn't demur when I moved the conversation up another gear. I told her exactly what I knew she wanted to hear. The deliciously dirty things I was doing to her. The forbidden fantasies she was unleashing on me. At first, she said almost nothing, but that didn't last. When the dam broke, it was as if we were playing a new Olympic sport of competitive arousal.

The thing about phone sex and cybersex is that anyone can be the perfect lover. I'd studied everything Allie had ever said to me about sex, pondered carefully the porn that turned her on. Because I was interested only in impressing her with how perfect a fit we were, I could give her everything she had ever wanted without having to consider for a moment whether or not it aroused me or turned me off. Women can fake it anywhere; men need to be invisible to achieve the same result. That first time on the phone, I really didn't care whether I came or not. What I was concerned with was keeping Allie on the hook.

That I did come with such intensity only confirmed for me how right I'd been to choose her.

We made the most of Jeffrey's absence.

What I hadn't bargained for was that term was almost over. Jeffrey was spending an increasing amount of time at home, marking exam papers, writing up his latest research papers. But in a funny kind of way, that worked to my advantage too. It meant we couldn't call each other as much as Allie wanted to. There's nothing like scarcity to push up the value of a commodity.

After three weeks of this, she was going crazy.

I didn't plan to feel this way, Larry. But all I can think about is being with you, in cyberspace or on the phone. I don't understand this; it's not like I suddenly stopped loving Jeffrey or anything. It's not that I want to leave him and run away with you. We both know that two writers under the same roof is a recipe for disaster. But whatever it is that's glowing between us needs resolution, and I don't see how we can have this unless we spend some time together. I know I'll see you in October in Washington at the convention, but that's not the right environment for us to find out what's really going on here.
A xxx

Darling Allie,
<that's not the right environment for us to find out what's really going on here.>
You're right. So here's what we do. You tell Jeffrey you've been invited to a conference in Europe to talk about your books. Make it somewhere he won't be desperate to visit, and make it on dates when he'd got something in his diary it would be impossible to cancel. I'll send you the air tickets and the hotel reservation, and you come over here. We'll have five days or so together. One way or another, we'll know where we're going.
I know I shouldn't say this, Allie. But I love you.
Larry

Of course, she couldn't resist. We settled on five days in Brussels. Now I had to start being very, very careful. There must never be any grounds for suspicion. I took the car over on the ferry from Harwich to the Hook of Holland and drove down to Brussels. I bought an air ticket in Allie's name in a busy travel agency, paying in cash. I made a hotel reservation, also in her name, and paid a deposit in cash. I FedExed the ticket and the hotel reservation to her from Brussels along with a letter I'd faked up on the computer, so that her story would hang together for Jeffrey's benefit.

The intervening two weeks were torture. It was easier for Allie; she'd already had a lot more than a taste of what it felt like to have your fantasies become reality. But the burning desire that had pushed me into this conspiracy was growing stronger in me day by day. She'd had satisfaction; mine was still to come, and the need ate at me like an incessant heartburn of the soul.

The night before she was due to fly out, I composed a very careful e-mail.

> Dearest Allie,
> I know you're going to think this is paranoid, but I'm thinking here of the future for you and Jeffrey. I know you're not certain what that future is going to be, but it's entirely possible you will want your relationship to continue.
> So it's important that he doesn't find anything while you're gone that might indicate to him that there is any reason for him to doubt your feelings.
> I know from what you've told me that you keep our exchange of e-mails in a separate folder in your comms program's filing cabinet.

What you need to do is delete the whole folder. I know you don't want to destroy our correspondence, but I've got everything on file here, and I'll send you a copy of it all as soon as you get home. I just don't think we should tempt fate. It has a horrible way of biting back.

What do you think?

Love, always,

Larry

Oh God, babe, you don't know what you're asking. I know deep down you're so right, but it feels like cutting out my heart to delete all the beautiful things you've said to me. (not to mention the down and dirty ones, heh heh heh)

I'm going to do it, though. Last thing before I leave. What I never told you is that I printed out all your e-mails to me. While Jeffrey's out at the gym this afternoon, I'm going to shred them. I hate to do it, but I know it makes sense.

Like the song says, I can't wait to meetchu . . .

Love, love, love,

A xxx

I only realised I'd been holding my breath when I got to the end of the e-mail. I couldn't help smiling. *Good girl, Allie*, I thought. Now there would be no obvious trace of me on her computer. Nothing for nosy Jeffery to find if he started looking for reasons why Allie had gone off sex with him.

That night, I made the crossing to Holland again. I booked myself into a hotel near the ferry port. I plugged my laptop into the phone socket and set it up so that it would make a <send and receive mail> call every seventy-three minutes until midnight. That way, there would be a record of me making phone calls from the room throughout the day, should I ever need to convince Jeffrey that I'd been nowhere near his beloved Allie. I took the stairs down and slipped out while the foyer was busy with a coach-load of pensioners from Ipswich.

I took my time driving down to Brussels. I was conscious of how edgy I was and I knew that could easily translate into the kind of bad driving that picks up a ticket from the traffic police. I arrived at the hotel around the same time Allie's flight was due to land. I found a legal parking slot about fifteen minutes' walk away and left the car there, carrying nothing with me but the laptop case containing a lightweight raincoat I'd bought in Holland. With cash, of course.

There was a busy bar on a corner opposite the hotel, and I wedged myself into a spot by the window where I could watch the entrance. I knew what she looked like now; although she'd always refused to send me a photograph, claiming I'd only be disappointed and wouldn't want to meet her, I'd finally tracked down an article on the internet from her local paper. They'd published a photograph of her at a book signing. As I'd thought, she wasn't beautiful. She wasn't ugly either; but you could see she'd have gone through her teens as a wallflower. The fat kid that nobody wants to dance with.

I'd been there about an hour when she climbed out of one of the regular stream of taxis. I watched as the bellboy took her suitcase, catching a glimpse of her nervous frown. I left it about ten minutes, then I called the hotel from the bar and asked for Ms James in my best American accent.

When I heard the familiar 'Hello?' my heart rate shot up.

I was so close now. I'd been rehearsing this scenario in my head for so long, the thought of it coming to fruition was enough to make me hard.

'It's me,' I said. 'I'm about twenty minutes away.'

'Oh God,' she said, her voice cracking. 'Larry, I'm so scared. I'm going to be a major disappointment.'

'No way,' I said. 'I know the woman inside. And she's beautiful. I'm so glad you made it.'

'Me too. Twenty minutes, you said?'

'Less, if I can make it.'

She chuckled. 'No. I need to shower and get into something a little more alluring.'

'Twenty minutes,' I said firmly.

'You're so masterful,' she teased.

'Believe it,' I said.

She opened the door so swiftly I wondered if she'd been standing behind it. I suppose if I'd been in love, it would have been a breathtaking sight. She was wearing a black lace basque with push-up cups. Her stockings were sheer and black, her heels high and spindly. She stood with one leg cocked at what's generally assumed to be a coquettish angle, one hand on hip, the other on the door. She'd done her best. It was as good as it was ever going to get, given what genetics had handed out to her.

Believe me, it wasn't what I saw that was reviving my erection. It was the realisation that all my careful planning had worked out in fact as precisely as it ever had in my fantasies.

Her smile was tentative, the ultimate oxymoron in the light of the brazen nature of her pose. I stepped forward and gently closed the door behind me. 'Wow,' I said.

'You mean it?'

I nodded, dropping my bag and moving into her. 'I mean it.' I buried my face in her hair. She hadn't had time to shower, and it had that musky, animal smell that women spend fortunes trying to erase. I wrapped one arm around her, easing her back towards the king-sized bed I'd specifically asked for when I booked the room. Her lips were all over my face as we inched backwards. I nibbled her ear, moaning softly. This time, there was no calculation. My response was for real.

She fell back on to the bed and I let myself fall with her, my knee between her thighs. I could feel her wetness through the fine wool of my trousers. Her hand was groping for my cock, pushing my jacket aside. With one hand, I reached for her face, pushing her hair back so I could look into her eyes.

With my free hand, I reached behind me and pulled the knife from the waistband of my trousers. As I plunged it into her side again and again, her hand closed convulsively against me.

I think I was coming as she died.

As I said, we'd done virtually everything before we met. But not quite.

The Road and the Miles to Dundee

I hate this dress. It's lemon yellow with blue roses and it makes my skin look like semolina pudding, my cheeks like dauds of strawberry jam in the middle of the plate. This dress, it's Bri-nylon and it cuts in under my arms and it makes me sweat. I hate the crackly white petticoat that's sewn in. It's like plastic, scratchy and rustly. You can hear me coming halfway across the town. Mostly, though, I hate it because it's a hand-me-down. It belonged to my cousin Morag whom I'm supposed to like because she's my cousin and she's only a year older than me, but I hate her too. She's a clipe, always telling tales. She's a Moaning Minnie. And she's boring. And I get the horrible clothes Auntie Betty makes for her after she's outgrown them. And they never fit because she's a beanpole and I'm not. But I have to wear them. According to my mum, they're too good to throw away. Me, I'd build a bonfire and set light to the lot of them.

It's my big cousin Senga's twenty-first, which is why I'm wearing the party dress. We're all crammed into my Auntie Jean's living-room, and the adults are all red in the face and cheery with the drink. This is my first grown-up party, and I'm supposed to be pleased that I've been allowed to come and stay up past my bedtime. But there's nothing to do and nobody to talk to. I can't even torment Morag because she's not here. Auntie Betty made her stay at home because it's too late for a big jessie like Morag to be up, even though she's eleven and I'm only ten. Next time I see her, I'll tell her how great it was. She willnae know it's a lie.

I'm that fed up I've made myself a den. I'm sitting under the table with a tumbler of lemonade and a bowl of crisps I sneaked away when nobody was looking. I've never had crisps like this before. They're sort of square and very yellow and if you look at them really close up, they've got lots of tiny wee bubbles under the surface. They don't even taste like crisps. When I suck them, they sort of burst on my tongue and taste of cheese and salt, not potatoes. The bag they came in said, 'Marks & Spencer Savoury Crisps', so I thought they'd be all right. I'm not really sure if I like them or not. But I'm bored, so I'm eating them just the same.

Somebody turns off the record player and now it's time for people to do their party pieces. Auntie Jean first, just as soon as she's finished telling off Uncle Tom for not refilling her rum and coke quick enough. She's always telling Uncle Tom off for something. I feel sorry for him. I thought it was only bairns that got picked on like she picks on him. I thought when you were a grown-up, folk stopped bothering you.

Anyway, Auntie Jean's got her rum and coke and she's away. Eyes shut, swaying a wee bit with the emotion. She always used to sing 'Grannie's Hielan' Hame', but lately she's taken to that Julie Rogers song, 'The Wedding'. Maybe she's trying to tell Senga something. Her voice is rusty with fags, but she belts it out all the same. 'And I can hear sweet voices singing, Ave Mar-ee-hee-haa.' Dad says when God was handing out voices, Auntie Jean was in the lavvy. When she finishes, everybody whoops and cheers. I don't know why, unless it's relief because it's over.

Then it's my dad. I squirm around under the table so I can

see him better. He plants his feet a wee bit apart and squares his shoulders in his good grey suit. I know what's coming. 'The Road and the Miles to Dundee' is his song. Nobody else would dare sing it. Apart from anything else, it would just make them look stupid, because my dad's got a great voice. He's as good as Kenneth McKellar. Everybody says so. He clears his throat and out comes that sweet voice that makes me feel like I'm snuggled up someplace safe and warm.

> *Cauld winter was howlin' o'er moor and o'er mountain*
> *And wild was the surge of the dark rolling sea,*
> *When I met about daybreak a bonnie young lassie,*
> *Wha asked me the road and the miles to Dundee.*

He's on the last verse when everything goes wrong. Without thinking about it, I've eased out from under the table to hear better. And that's when that evil witch Auntie Betty spots me. My dad's just coming to the end of the song when she bellows like a bullock. 'My God, have you ett that whole bowl of crisps yoursel'? Nae wonder you've got all that puppy fat on you.'

I want to die. Instead of looking at my dad, everybody's looking at me. The last note dies away, and though a few folk are clapping, mostly they're eyeing up the yellow lemon dress straining at the seams. I can see them thinking, 'Greedy wee shite', as clearly as if they had cartoon thought bubbles over their heads. I want to shout out and tell them I just look fat because it's not my dress.

There's a horrible moment of hush. Then suddenly my dad's feet appear in front of my face. 'Leave the bairn alone,

Betty,' he says in a different voice from the one we've all been listening to. This one's hard and quiet, the one I know never to argue with.

But Auntie Betty's stupid as well as evil. 'Jim, I'm only speaking for her own good,' she says, and I can hear exactly where Morag gets her slimy ways fi'.

'Betty,' my dad says, 'You've always been an interfering bitch. Now leave my bairn alone.'

Auntie Betty flushes scarlet and retreats, muttering something nobody's listening to. There's a flurry of movement and Uncle Don launches into 'The Mucking o' Geordie's Byre'. My dad drops to the floor beside me, says nothing, puts his hand over mine.

My hero.

> *Says I, 'My young lassie, I canna' weel tell ye*
> *The road and the distance I canna' weel gie.*
> *But if you'll permit me tae gang a wee bittie,*
> *I'll show ye the road and the miles to Dundee.'*
>
> *At once she consented and gave me her arm,*
> *Ne'er a word did I speir wha the lassie micht be,*
> *She appeared like an angel in feature and form,*
> *As she walked by my side on the road to Dundee.*

* * *

I'm off to university in a couple of days. I'm really excited, but I'm a bit scared too. I'm off to England. I've only ever been there twice before – the first time, a holiday in Blackpool when I was eleven, the second my university interview.

Both times, I felt like I'd been transported to another planet. Now my life as an alien is about to begin, and I can't wait to get away and dive into this new world. I can be anybody I want to be. I can make myself up from scratch.

But for now, I'm still trapped in who I've always been. This time next week, I'll be in the shadow of Oxford's dreaming spires, drinking coffee with intellectuals, talking about politics and ideas and literature. Tonight, though, I'm at Dysart Miners' Welfare for my cousin Senga's spree. She's marrying an Englishman. 'I don't suppose they have sprees in England,' I say to him.

'No,' he says. There's something about the way he says it that makes me think he's another one who's feeling like his life as an alien is only just beginning.

The show of presents is at the far end of the hall, a row of trestle tables covered in white paper, groaning under the weight of china, linen, glassware and the strange assortment of things people think newlyweds need for a proper start in life. There's a whole subsection entirely devoted to Pyrex casseroles. My cousin Derry whispers to me that Hutt's department store had a special offer on Pyrex last month, that's why there are twenty-three of them on display. 'Do you think they'll be able to swap them?' I ask.

'Christ, I hope so,' he says. 'Otherwise we'll all be getting Pyrex for Christmas.'

The demarcation lines are clearly drawn. The women sit at tables round the perimeter of the hall, leaving a space in the middle for the dancing. The men congregate round the long bar that occupies most of one side of the room. I'm already getting the hard stare from Auntie Betty and her cronies for standing with the men at the bar, drinking underage pints and smoking. Morag is staring wistfully across at me, like she wishes she had the nerve to come and join me and Derry and Senga's fiancé. But she won't budge. She hasn't got a rebellious molecule in her body.

The band's been playing a wee while now, and a few folk have been dancing, but nothing much is happening. 'Is it no' time for a wee song, Jim?' one of the other men asks my dad.

'Aye, you're probably right. I'll away up and have a word with the bandleader.' It's a grandiose term for the leader of the trio of accordion, drums and guitar that have been serenading us with a competent if uninspired selection of Scottish standards and pop songs from the previous decade. But my dad walks up to the stage anyway and leans over the accordionist, his mouth close to the wee bald man's ear.

When they finish their rendition of 'The Bluebell Polka', my dad steps up to the microphone. 'Ladies and gentlemen, the band has kindly agreed that they'll accompany anybody who wants to give us a song. So if you don't mind, I'll start off the proceedings.' And he's off. The familiar words float above the band and he treats us to his usual graceful rendition.

But tonight, I'm not in the mood. I'm not daddy's wee lassie any more. I'm a young woman on the threshold of her life, and I don't want to acquiesce quietly to anything. He finishes the song and, by popular demand, gives us an encore of 'Ae Fond Kiss'.

By the time he gets back to the bar, Auntie Jean is up there, belting out 'The Wedding' with all the smug complacency of a woman who has got the difficult daughter boxed off on the road to the aisle. My dad takes a welcome swallow of his lager and smiles at me.

I scowl in return. 'Does it not strike you as a wee bit hypocritical, you singing that song?' I say.

He looks baffled. 'What?'

'It's all about a man who takes pity on a lassie who's trying to get to Dundee. Right? He helps her. With no thought of anything in return. Right?' I demand.

'Aye,' he says cautiously. The last year or two have taught him caution is a good policy when it comes to crossing verbal swords with me. I've learned a lot from the school debating society, and even more from the students in Edinburgh I hang out with at weekends.

'And you don't find anything hypocritical in that?'

'No,' he says. 'He does the right thing, the fellow in the song.'

'So how come you won't pick up hitchhikers, then?' I say. Game, set and match.

> *At length wi' the Howe o' Strathmartine behind us,*
> *The spires o' the toon in full view we could see,*
> *She said 'Gentle Sir, I can never forget ye*
> *For showing me far on the road to Dundee'.*
>
> *I took the gowd pin from the scarf on my bosom*
> *And said 'Keep ye this in remembrance o' me'*
> *Then bravely I kissed the sweet lips o' the lassie,*
> *E'er I parted wi' her on the road to Dundee.*

*   *   *

I'm staying with my friend Antonia and her husband, who have a house on the shores of Lake Champlain, a long finger of water that forms part of the border between Vermont and New York State. Antonia and I became friends at Oxford, in spite of the difference in our backgrounds. She was a diplomat's daughter, educated at public school, born to privilege and position. And it didn't matter a damn because we were equals in the things that mattered.

We're having a good time. This feels like the life I've always wanted. My first book is due to be published in a week's time, I'm travelling the world, young, free and single, and I have appropriated Antonia's sense of entitlement with not a premonition of what might change that. I'm swimming in the chilly dark waters of Lake Champlain when it happens, though I'm oblivious to it the time. We come out of the water and run up to the house, our only thought how soon we can get dried off and settle in front of the log fire with a glass of good malt whisky.

It's the middle of the night when I find out my life has changed irrevocably. I drift out of sleep, woken by a distant phone ringing. I turn over and set my compass for unconsciousness when Antonia is suddenly standing in front of me, her face crumpled and distressed. 'The phone . . . it's for you.' I can't make sense of this but I roll out of bed and go downstairs anyway. Her husband is standing mute, the receiver held out to me.

The voice on the other end is familiar. 'I'm awful sorry, lassie,' says Uncle Tom. 'It's your dad. He was playing bowls. He walked out on the green to play the final of the tournament. And he just dropped down dead.' His voice keeps going, but I can't make out the words.

Later that day, I'm walking in the rain in Central Park. Antonia has organised everything; a flight from Burlington to New York, then a night flight back to Scotland via Paris. I've packed my bags, but I've still got four hours to kill. So I buy my first packet of cigarettes in years and walk. Smoke and rain, good excuses for a wet face and red eyes. The dye in my passport runs as I get soaked to the skin; for years, I can't escape remembrance of this day every time I travel abroad.

It's taken them a couple of days to track me down, so I don't get back till the day of the funeral. The crematorium is packed, standing-room only for a man so many people loved. The minister's doing a good job – he knew my dad, so he understands the need to celebrate a life as well as mourn a death. He actually makes us laugh, and I think of my dad watching all this from somewhere else and maybe realising how much his life meant.

Back at the house, after the formal funeral purvey, it's family only. I'm in the kitchen with our Senga making potted meat sandwiches. I feel dazed. I'm not sure whether it's grief or jetlag or what. I'm taking the bread knife to a tall stack of sandwiches, cutting them into neat triangles, when Auntie Betty barges into the kitchen. She puts a hand on my shoulder and says, 'Are you awful upset about your dad, then?'

It's a question so crass I can't believe she's uttered it. I feel Senga's hand gently easing the bread knife from mine. Just as well, really. I stare mutely at Auntie Betty, wishing with my whole heart that it was her burned to ash instead of my dad.

Senga says, 'If you don't mind, Auntie Betty, there's not really room for three people in here and we need to get the sandwiches done.'

Auntie Betty edges backwards. 'Right enough,' she says. 'I just thought I'd come and tell you Simon's going to give us a wee song.'

Simon is the late baby, born when Morag was twelve. There has never been a child more beautiful, more intelligent, more gifted. Well, that's what Auntie Betty thinks. Personally, I prefer another set of adjectives – spoilt, arrogant, average. His thin, reedy tenor makes me yearn for Auntie Jean singing 'The Wedding'.

'Aye,' Betty continues. 'He's going to give us "The Road and the Miles to Dundee".'

I feel the blood draining from my face and the room loses focus. I push her out of the way and head for the front door, grabbing my jacket as I run. I tear from the house and jump into the car, not caring that I've had more whisky than the law allows drivers. At first, I'm not thinking about where I'm going, but my heart knows what it needs, and it's not my cousin Simon murdering my father's favourite song. I drive out of town and up into the hills. These days, you can drive almost all the way up Falkland Hill. But it didn't use to be like that. The first time I climbed it was the night before my sixth birthday. My mum wanted me out of the way so she could ice the cake, and my dad took me up the hill. It felt like a mountain to my child's legs; it felt like achievement. We stood on the top, looking down at Fife, my world, spread beneath our feet like a magic carpet.

Now, twenty-six years later, I'm here again. I want music. I finger the tape of my dad singing that one of his friends from the Bowhill People's Burns Club's concert party pressed into my hand as I left the crematorium. 'I made a wee compilation for you,' he said, his eyes damp with sorrow.

But I'm not ready for this. Instead, I slam the Mozart Requiem into the tape player, roll down the windows, turn the volume up full and stand on the hillside, staring out at the blurry view. I know the world is still at my feet.

The difference is that today, I don't want it.

> *So here's to the lassie, I ne'er can forget her,*
> *And ilka young laddie that's listening to me,*
> *O never be sweer to convoy a young lassie*
> *Though it's only to show her the road to Dundee.*

* * *

I'm thirty thousand feet above somewhere. I don't much care where. I'm flying to a festival to read from my work in a country I can't point to on a map. I'm flying away from the ending of the relationship I never expected to die. My life feels ragged and wrecked, my heart torn and trampled. It's as if the last dozen years have been folded up tight like tissue paper, turning into a hard lump that could stick in my throat and choke me.

I take out the book I've brought as a bulwark against the strangling gyre of my thoughts. Ali Smith's *The Whole Story and Other Stories*. I chose it deliberately in preference to a novel because I can't actually concentrate for long enough to manage more than bite-sized chunks.

A few stories in, I start reading one called 'Scottish Love Songs'. It's magical and strange, tragic and funny, but most of all, it's an affirmation of the power and endurance of love. A bitter irony that I'm far from immune to. I'm bearing up well until the pipers in the story start playing 'The Road and the Miles to Dundee'. Then I become that person that nobody wants to sit next to on the plane, the one with the fat tears rolling down her cheeks and the trumpeting nose-blowing that shocks even the screaming toddler in the next row into silence.

Two nights later, I'm lying in a bed in a city in the middle of Europe, limbs entangled with a virtual stranger. We're in that charmed place between satisfactory sex and the recognition that we probably don't have much to say to each other. I don't know why, but I start to tell her about the incident on the plane, and all the other memories associated with 'The Road and the Miles to Dundee'. I don't expect much response; I recall once writing that casual lovers are like domestic pets – you can almost believe they understand every word you say.

But I'm pleasantly surprised. She shifts her long legs so she can more readily face me, pushes her tawny hair out of her eyes and frowns in concentration. At one point, when I pause, searching for the next point in the narrative, her hand moves to my hip and she says, 'Go on. This is interesting.'

I come to the end of what I have to say and she traces my mouth with a fingertip. 'Sad,' she says. Then shakes her head. 'No, strike that. Sad's too small a word. Too simple.'

But simplification is what I need. I suddenly understand that I want to strip away every association from this damn song except the sweetness of my father's voice. I don't know how to express this, but somehow, this woman grasps the essence without being told. 'It's a love song,' she says. 'You need to remember that. You need to replace the bad connections with good ones.'

'Easier said than done,' I sigh. I want to change the subject, so I choose something else to occupy our mouths. It's sweet, this encounter. It doesn't touch the core of my pain, but it reminds me that sooner or later, there will be mitigation.

Three days later, we detach from each other in the departure lounge, heading for different provincial airports. We've made no plans to meet again, mostly because I've headed her off at the pass every time.

I'm only home an hour when there's a ring at the doorbell. I'm not expecting anyone, but of all the people I'm not expecting, the florist would come high on the list. But she's there, presenting me with a dozen yellow roses. Puzzled, I check they're really for me and not the woman next door. The florist smiles at my distrust. 'No, they're really for you,' she says. 'There's a card. I hope I got the spelling right.'

I close the door and walk slowly through to the kitchen. I wriggle the card free from the cellophane wrapping and tear open the envelope. I read the words, and I can't keep the big silly smile from my face. '*O never be sweer to convoy a young lassie, Though it's only to show her the road to Dundee.*'

The phone's ringing, and I have a funny feeling it's going to be a voice asking for directions.